ELENA AGAINST THE WORLD

Everyone informed Elena that her only proper course of action was to wed Lord Harcourt.

Her strong-willed parents, Lord and Lady Tyndale, found Harcourt an emminently suitable suitor in terms of wealth and station.

Her personal maid, Jane, considered Harcourt quite the most handsome gentleman in all the realm.

Lord Harcourt himself was willing to defy his own mother's wishes and dash the hopes of the beauty who was pledged to be his bride in order to lead Elena to the altar.

But Elena vowed that no one in the world could induce her to give herself to this monster who wore the mask of a perfect mate—and she would, she insisted, rather break her heart than break her word. . . .

THE UNWELCOME SUITOR

More Delightful Regency Romances from SIGNET

(0451)
- ☐ THE ACCESSIBLE AUNT by Vanessa Gray. (126777—$2.25)
- ☐ THE DUKE'S MESSENGER by Vanessa Gray. (118685—$2.25)*
- ☐ THE DUTIFUL DAUGHTER by Vanessa Gray. (090179—$1.75)*
- ☐ THE WICKED GUARDIAN by Vanessa Gray. (083903—$1.75)
- ☐ RED JACK'S DAUGHTER by Edith Layton. (129148—$2.25)*
- ☐ THE MYSTERIOUS HEIR by Edith Layton. (126793—$2.25)
- ☐ THE DISDAINFUL MARQUIS by Edith Layton. (124480—$2.25)*
- ☐ THE DUKE'S WAGER by Edith Layton. (120671—$2.25)*
- ☐ A SUITABLE MATCH by Joy Freeman. (117735—$2.25)*

*Prices slightly higher in Canada

Buy them at your local bookstore or use this convenient coupon for ordering.

NEW AMERICAN LIBRARY,
P.O. Box 999, Bergenfield, New Jersey 07621

Please send me the books I have checked above. I am enclosing $_____
(please add $1.00 to this order to cover postage and handling). Send check or money order—no cash or C.O.D.'s. Prices and numbers are subject to change without notice.

Name _____

Address _____

City _____ State _____ Zip Code _____

Allow 4-6 weeks for delivery.
This offer is subject to withdrawal without notice.

THE UNWELCOME SUITOR

by Marjorie DeBoer

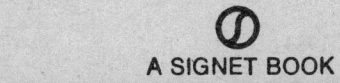

A SIGNET BOOK
NEW AMERICAN LIBRARY

NAL BOOKS ARE AVAILABLE AT QUANTITY DISCOUNTS
WHEN USED TO PROMOTE PRODUCTS OR SERVICES. FOR
INFORMATION PLEASE WRITE TO PREMIUM MARKETING
DIVISION, NEW AMERICAN LIBRARY, 1633 BROADWAY,
NEW YORK, NEW YORK 10019.

Copyright © 1984 by Marjorie Rockwell DeBoer

All rights reserved

SIGNET TRADEMARK REG. U.S.PAT. OFF. AND FOREIGN COUNTRIES
REGISTERED TRADEMARK—MARCA REGISTRADA
HECHO EN CHICAGO, U.S.A.

SIGNET, SIGNET CLASSIC, MENTOR, PLUME, MERIDAN and NAL BOOKS
are published by New American Library, 1633 Broadway,
New York, New York 10019

First Printing, August, 1984

1 2 3 4 5 6 7 8 9

PRINTED IN THE UNITED STATES OF AMERICA

1

That afternoon in early May, Elena Tyndale left the house without telling her parents, Sir John and Lady Theresa, or any of the servants, and set out for Wood Walton Fen, alone. Her secretiveness was not planned or especially defiant. It was simply that neither her father's pity nor her mother's concern could have calmed the uneasiness that seized her whenever she considered her imminent departure for London the next day.

And so Elena sought open air and solitude instinctively, as a thirsty person seeks water while journeying across a desert. She needed the bursting trees and birdcalls to remind her, once again, that grief was not forever, that death always gave birth to life, mysteriously, endlessly.

In the four years since Sir John, forced by ill health to give up his diplomatic post in Vienna, had moved his wife and daughter back to the ancestral home in Huntingdonshire, Elena had grown to love Tyndale Green and the surrounding countryside. The unkempt, tangled beauty of the garden; the picturesque stone bridge that spanned a shallow stream; the clover-sweet, sun-warmed meadow, inhabited by buzzing insects and drowsy sheep; the cool damp-moss smell of the woods which led to the wild fens along the estate's boundary—all fed her spirit, which had smothered for years in the circumscribed propriety of Europe's capitals. London, another capital, would be no different, she supposed. She had never before been there.

She had protested that she was not yet ready for society. But her objections had not moved Lady Theresa, whose firm hand in the matter of her only child's upbringing had not slackened with the passing of Elena's twentieth birthday. If anything it had tightened, thanks to Elena's incredible conduct of the past autumn.

Lady Theresa had nobly shouldered part of the blame for that herself. Had she not allowed her daughter to go to the Cheltenham Spa with the Duke and Duchess of Malvern, the disaster never would have occurred. But how could she have foreseen that Elena would elope one fine night from a fancy-dress ball with Captain Rodney Farnsworth, whom she had known exactly three weeks? Or that they would drive recklessly in the captain's curricle all the way to Gretna Green and there be married by a Scottish justice in a scandalous, barely legal ceremony?

"Could you not realize it was quite wrong, even if this captain was the Duchess's nephew? Did I not bring you up better than that?" Lady Theresa had reproached her.

Yes, Elena had replied with an outward show of repentance. For of course she had been brought up in the best traditions of English gentility and Anglican morality, and she had known that she was breaking those traditions. But she had hoped—indeed, had expected—it would all come right, once her parents had met Captain Farnsworth and seen how perfectly suited they were for each other. And they had acted in haste only because they had so little time, with Rodney on leave from Army duty only two weeks longer.

She could not utter the obvious—that she had been besotted with love for him, that being with Rodney Farnsworth had made her forget decorum and duty. Charming, handsome, daring, *alive*, he had knocked sense from her head and replaced it with adoration. They had been married just five days when he had been killed.

Elena had retreated back home in a dazed grief that could not comprehend shame. She was *not* ashamed; she would do it again in a minute. She could not tell her mother that, either.

For eight months she had been allowed the luxury of mourning in semiseclusion. But now Lady Theresa feared she would slip into a decline if she remained at home and moped any longer. More to the point, she feared Elena would never make a good match if she were not forced into opportunities to meet eligible gentlemen soon, for since her shocking loss Elena seemed content with solitude and could rarely be persuaded to attend even the modest social affairs of the surrounding shire. When her sister, Lady Winifred Cunnington, sympathizing with Lady Theresa's dilemma by post, had volunteered to guide the girl through the intricacies of the London Season, it seemed an opportunity sent by heaven.

Lady Theresa had hoped for some time that Sir John might eventually be well enough to take his family to London, so she could personally supervise Elena's debut, but the miracle had not happened. Sir John's lung condition, though improved since his return to rural England, would, his doctor insisted, only worsen in London, notorious for its choking, coke-grimed fogs. Lady Theresa would not chance it.

Her husband came first, as he always had, and no amount of persuasion would have convinced her to accompany Elena to London without him.

Elena did not in the least resent her mother's attitude, for she, too, adored her handsome father with his gentle, self-deprecatory wit. She had often preferred his quiet company to that of her mother, who, no matter how devoted, tended to hover and fuss about little things. And when it became clear that Sir John also thought she needed the Season in London, Elena stopped protesting, except for one glaring objection that she felt bound to raise.

"But, Mama, I have been married. My true role should be that of a widow. It will certainly be deceptive if I am presented in Society as an eligible young maiden."

The marriage had been annulled, Lady Theresa reminded her quickly, passing over the implications of Elena's reference to "maiden" in such a way that she dared not refer to it again. Thanks to the circumstances and the captain's untimely demise, it had been possible to successfully petition the Church, stating in effect that Elena had been forced to marry against her will. Furthermore, the matter had been hushed up. Only the immediate family and the Duke and Duchess, who, deeply regretful of their part in introducing Elena to the captain, had agreed to keep silent, knew there had been an elopement at all. Instead, it had been given out that Elena had taken ill while at Cheltenham and had returned home the day after the fateful assembly ball.

She had had eight months to grieve over him, Lady Theresa reminded her. Now she must put him out of her mind and think of her future.

But I'm not a maiden, Elena thought as she entered the woods that marched across the northernmost extension of Sir John's property. Annulment is not a magic word that can erase what I experienced during those five wonderful days. I'm a woman now; I know what it is to love a man. It's a little like taking too much wine—you lose your head as well as your heart. It's wonderfully giddy and beyond understanding. And I shall never know it again, now Rodney's gone.

Recently she had been able to think of him without experiencing the stabbing pain of the first few months. But as the tall oaks closed in about her, the old anguish returned in double measure. She shivered, clutched her cloak about her, and tried to direct her thoughts elsewhere, but it was no use. They persisted in recalling again that dreadful night when Rodney had died.

The driving rain and the lame horse, the seedy inn where they had been forced to seek shelter, the difficulty in persuading sullen servants to supply them with fresh bedding, hot water, a light supper, a fire in their chamber's hearth . . . But although she had finally been lulled by warmth and food and was ready for sleep, Rodney, overset by all the difficulties they had encountered, had said he must go to the taproom for a while.

She would probably never know exactly what happened, but she would surely never forget the horror of that night—a pounding at the door of the bedchamber, waking her from a fog of sleep, and then the unbelievable sight of Rodney, unconscious and bloodied, being carried past her and deposited on the bed amid the landlord's bewildered explanations. The captain and another man, apparently friends, had been drinking together when their conversation had suddenly erupted into a fight. He had not seen the crippling blow.

After the first incredulous cry of disbelief, Elena had been afflicted with a numb terror that forbade her even speaking. Nevertheless, though shivering and distraught, she had helped the landlord's wife apply a cold poultice to check the blood streaming from Rodney's cut eye. A surgeon was coming, the woman kept saying. The other gentleman, unhurt, had gone to fetch him.

Suddenly Rodney stirred and murmured her name, and his fingers gripped hers. She leaned close, tears blurring her eyes. "For you . . ." he whispered, recognizing her. Then, like a demented man he raised up and burst out, "That damned McKean! I'll kill . . ." Just as abruptly his gaze became fixed and his head dropped back to the bed like a stone. Elena watched, horrified, as blood filled the poultice, gushed down his cheek from under the dressing, and poured onto the pillow as if from a burst dam. The fingers clutching hers went limp.

The surgeon arrived half an hour later and pronounced what they already knew. The man who had killed Rodney never reappeared. Elena's father, receiving word of her whereabouts, came to fetch her home. Sick with shock and grief, she paid no attention to what, if any, investigation was made into the matter. Her loss was all that counted.

Tomorrow she would be put under Aunt Winifred's wing in London. Elena could understand her mother's anxiety about her future, but she doubted she would ever again be open to love. The prospect of another marriage—brilliant or otherwise—repelled her. Why must it be everyone's favorite solution for what ailed her? Waves of rebellion hastened her stride. She would have broken into a run had not the clinging muslin of her ankle-length skirt forbidden it.

THE UNWELCOME SUITOR

Once out of the wood she followed a faint path onto a rise of low bushes and fern, and stopped to take in her favorite view. Wood Walton Fen shimmered before her, tumultuous with new life. Oaks and willows stretched newly green arches above the tall grasses and reeds and sallow bushes. The pungent scents of fish and damp peat vied with those of the emerging vegetation beneath her feet. Wild duck and geese, blue hawks, bitterns, and grasshopper warblers filled the air with mating calls and joyous flight. Away to her left, the road to Huntingdon, cutting through the woods, crossed a stream by way of an old wooden bridge so narrow that two bullock carts dared not pass on it.

Beyond the fen diaphanous clouds refracted the sun's light into distinct rays. Their pale slanted shafts told her it was teatime and Lady Theresa would be expecting her. Still she lingered, breathing in the fresh wild odors that, by tomorrow evening, would be only memory.

A few moments later she realized her solitude had been invaded. A figure was following the trail through the bracken, coming toward her. Shielding her eyes against the horizon's brightness, she finally identified a man, dressed in top boots and leathers, high-collared blue jacket, hatless. The sun glinted on the metal grip of his riding crop, which he was flicking impatiently—or was it angrily?—from one side of the path to the other.

Her first impulse was to avoid the stranger, as she had avoided everyone but her family all winter. But then curiosity stirred, riveting her to the hillock. He was taking the incline with youthful, athletic strides, and his thick curly hair gleamed like copper in the sun. As he came closer, she noticed that his neckcloth was soiled and the sleeve of his jacket ripped.

Still closer and she could make out his features: heavy black brows, a bold determined chin, and lean cheeks flushed with the exertion of his rapid stride. A handsome face in spite of his frown. A strong, almost overpowering face. She nearly turned and ran.

But he had seen her and waved an arm, compelling her to stay and address him. He stopped some ten feet away. "Good afternoon, madam," he called.

"Good afternoon, sir," she returned. Gazing at him resolutely, she noticed again the dirt, the rip, and a light smudge on his forehead. "Have you met with a mishap?"

"A mishap? More like a disaster. My horse took a tumble. I'm afraid both his forelegs are broken and I shall have to shoot him."

"Oh, surely not!" she cried out.

His black eyebrows shot up. "Surely not? Why not, pray? Have you some magic formula to restore him?"

She flushed. "I—I only meant, 'tis a pity."

His eyes, which seemed to reflect the green-gold-brown of the day, glinted with angry frustration. "Aye, that it is. Would you be kind enough to direct me to some nearby cottage or other . . ."

Dropping her gaze from his face, she saw for the first time that blood had darkened the ripped fabric of his jacket sleeve. "Why, you've been injured! Come, sir, I live just the other side of the wood. This is the property of Sir John Tyndale. Our housekeeper will attend to you."

"I'll tend myself later," he returned brusquely. "Now, I need some sort of shooting iron since it's too far to go back afoot for my own. Have you a gamekeeper by chance?"

The lack of courtesy with which he responded to

THE UNWELCOME SUITOR

her Good Samaritan impulses vexed her. She swallowed a stinging retort and said curtly, "Certainly. I'll take you to his cottage, and if he's not there, we'll go to the house."

"I'm much obliged to you, madam."

She inclined her head and turned to lead him back through the woods. Old Will might very well be sitting at his hearth about now, since it was teatime, but she knew he would not be happy about an interruption.

Though their single-file progress on the narrow path would have made any conversation uphill work, Elena felt unaccountably constrained by the silence. She felt the gaze of those saffron-dappled eyes boring into her back and remembered his sarcastic response to her pity, his abrupt, direct manner. Most of all she was aware of the sheer masculine vigor of his body, the sound of his boots crushing old leaves and brush, echoing right behind her. The back of her neck tingled as if he had reached out and touched it.

She thought of asking his name, his connections, the reason for his presence on her father's property, but she had not done so at first and asking now would be awkward and inappropriate, intruding on the urgency of the situation.

Old Will was past seventy, gnarled and bent like his favorite bur oak, touchy and independent when it came to his province, the woods and grounds, and still reputed to have the sharpest eyes and steadiest gun hand in the shire. He sat on the stoop in front of his door, balancing his chair on two legs against the rough plastered wall of the cottage, sipping his "brew," as he always called it. The ingredients, other than ale, were a mystery to Elena.

Will had been watching their approach, and by the time they were before him he had put his mug on the stoop, settled the chair on all fours, and stood beside it in respect for her presence. This did not fool Elena. Servant Old Will might be but, as her father was fond of saying, far from subservient.

"I'm sorry to trouble you, Will," she said, "but this gentleman's horse has met with an accident and . . ."

"The loan of a fowling piece is all I need," the stranger explained. "And then I shan't bother you further."

Old Will grunted and glanced from the man to Elena and back again. "D'ye want I should go wi' 'im, Miss Elena, to bring back t'gun? Because the old knee's a mite troublesome today, but I'll go if ye want."

"Never mind, Will. I'll accompany him myself and return the gun to you." She spoke the words soothingly, thoughtlessly, then turned to the stranger. "So you needn't make the trip twice, sir. Unless, of course, I can persuade you to receive aid . . ."

"It's nothing," he said. "I would, of course, have returned the gun as soon as possible, but I am in some haste today."

"But now you must travel afoot."

"It's no great distance, I assure you."

While they argued, Old Will had limped into the cottage. Now he returned with a double-barreled shotgun which he laboriously loaded. When he proffered the shot pouch, the stranger declined. "Two will be more than adequate, thank you." He turned back down the path without waiting to see if Elena followed.

"Mum," Old Will said softly, "to my way o' thinkin', ye shouldna do a servant's job. Stay 'ere, an' I'll fetch Tim fra' the stables to bring back t'gun."

"It will take too long to fetch him," Elena said impatiently, looking after the man's receding figure.

THE UNWELCOME SUITOR 15

"Then I'll send 'im after, mum, t'come back wi' ye. An', by the bye, tell the master where ye be off to."

"I don't even know where the horse was injured."

" 'E'll find the spot," the old man said stubbornly as he stumped off in the direction of the stables.

Elena shrugged to herself, caught up her skirts, and hurried up the path after the man. When she neared him, he said, without turning to look at her, "I thought you much too tenderhearted to see a horse shot. Or do you still hope to mend him?"

"No, indeed, I only came to make your task more convenient," Elena said tartly. He did not reply. They were silent again, she behind him this time until they reached the rise where they had met. "How far?" she asked.

"Maybe half a mile. Have you walking boots on?"

She flushed. She had, but it was incredibly forward of him to mention such a thing. "You haven't introduced yourself, sir," she said pointedly.

"Nor have you."

"I told you who I am."

But he continued on without answering her. She followed, wishing she had ordered Will to accompany him as he should have done, bad knee or no bad knee. The stranger's reticence and his lack of manners were becoming ominous. Will had warned her it wasn't fitting for her to be on a lonely path with a strange man. Now, her heart suddenly racing, she realized how utterly improper it was. She could only pray they came upon the horse soon and the bloody deed was accomplished and she could be quit of him!

The downhill slope of the path leveled out onto a low-lying meadow that was separated from the fen by a narrow dike. The stranger's mount, a bay with a white-streaked face, had given up the struggle to stand and now lay on his side near the dike. His flanks heaved, his nostrils were distended in pain, and foam flecked his great black lips. Hearing their approach, he strained to raise his head.

"Oh!" Elena cried out in pity. The man merely raised the gun to his shoulder, cautioned her to stand back, took aim, and fired. The shot caught the horse between the eyes. His head shuddered and grew rigid, then slowly relaxed and found final rest in the tall grass.

Tearing her eyes from the awful sight, she looked at her companion's face and saw that his jaw was clenched against emotion. He lowered the gun with a shuddering sigh. "Well—there. It had to be done." He walked over to the dead animal. "I shall, of course, see to the removal of the body." He discharged the second barrel into the ground before turning to hand her the gun. "For safety's sake," he said.

"You don't think I know how to handle a gun," she objected, taking it in two hands and looking at it dubiously.

"Do you?" His eyebrows rose, quizzical, wry.

"No, but you might have asked."

He laughed. His mirth was a greater shock to her than his previous brusqueness had been. "You have been most helpful," he assured her, a cordial note entering his voice for the first time. "Thank you again, Miss . . ."

"Miss Tyndale, of course," she supplied. "And you are . . . ?"

He gazed at her a long moment, as though she were a bird in a cage that he might properly study at will. And like some just-captured wild thing, she returned his stare as though mesmerized. He seemed to be really seeing her for the first time, and she remembered that people thought her black curls (though surely disheveled now) and long-lashed violet eyes and slender-bowed mouth beautiful. But his gaze was more thoughtful than admiring, and when it softened, as though he had somehow seen into her bruised heart, a flush spread over her cheeks.

At last—it seemed an age—he bowed very correctly and said, "Lawrence MacLean, at your service."

An unaccountable tremor danced through her body. "Are you in the neighborhood long, Mr. MacLean?" She hoped the question sounded like mere courtesy, that he could not know she suddenly thirsted for a straightforward answer. But then she made a mull of it by adding, "Perhaps we shall meet again."

"I hope we shall, indeed, Miss Tyndale," he replied with warmth. "But it worries me to see you so far from home and unaccompanied. If I were not pressed for time . . ."

"Pray don't concern yourself, sir," she said quickly. "I know the area well, and besides, one of our stable boys is sure to find me soon."

He bowed again. "Until next time, then, Miss Tyndale."

She inclined her head wordlessly and watched him turn and stride across the meadow toward the Huntingdon Road. She still knew nothing about him.

It was not until she reentered the wood, having already caught sight of Tim hurrying to meet her, that the sound of his name made sudden terrible connection with a name that had echoed in her brain for eight months: "That damned McKean . . ."

But, no, it couldn't have been. Why should she connect a stranger in Huntingdonshire with the villain who had dealt the death blow to Rodney in an obscure inn far to the north? The name was only similar. Ridiculous suspicion, doubtless born of her long self-imposed isolation from society. Perhaps her mother was right, after all, and a Season in London was exactly what she needed. Finding a husband wasn't of interest to her, but a little gaiety would be a welcome change.

2

Lady Winifred and Lord Geoffrey Cunnington lived on Queen Anne Street just above Cavendish Square. Their home had been built by Lord Cunnington's grandfather, the second Baron Cunnington, when the area was new. Nothing about the interior of the early Georgian house of white stone had been altered in the fifty years since. Worn carpets, draperies, upholstery, and bed curtains were always replaced by especially ordered ones of identical pattern. The paint and wall hangings, even when redone, remained the same color. The house was gloomy and ill-lit, a shortcoming that, Lady Cunnington had supposed upon her marriage twenty-five years before, surely might have been altered without doing violence to tradition. But she had not bargained on the second baron, who continued to live in the house and to whom change was anathema. On Elena's arrival, the house remained much as it had half a century before, much to Lady Cunnington's disgust.

"Still, it is just possible," she told her niece hopefully as she poured tea in the upstairs sitting room, "*if* I go about it carefully, I shall be able now to convince Geoffrey to at least do a little redecorating, as celebration for his at last achieving the title.

Surely I deserve it after so many years. The second baron was ninety-two when he died last winter. I'm sure it is marvelous to live so long, but I must confess, my dear Elena, that it has been a trial to live in his house all our married life. I think even Geoffrey would agree with me."

Elena, properly impressed by the difficulty of spending one's married life under the roof of an aged in-law, agreed that the rooms were gloomy. Nevertheless, her aunt's welcome had cheered her. She was being addressed as a sensible equal, not as a wayward child. Aunt Winifred, a large, good-looking woman whose sense of propriety was leavened with compassion and common sense, had made no mention of the elopement or its climax. Her perfect aplomb, her apparently innate knowledge of the fitness of things, seemed an integral part of her, reinforced by her social position but not a consequence of it.

Elena passed her first two days in London feeling somewhat adrift, as though she were recovering from a long, serious illness. At the same time she was unusually alive to the charm of the spring weather— the mild breezes, the vivid, precisely ordered flower beds in the squares, the comfort of taking tea and watercress sandwiches on the veranda in the late-afternoon sun, surrounded by potted palms and geraniums, listening with half her attention to her aunt's chatter while the other half took in the cacophony of bird song in the bushes behind the house. Her mind was quite empty of pain, and she thought it might very well remain that way so long as nothing was demanded of her. And for several days nothing was, except fittings for new clothes which Lady Theresa had authorized and whose acquisition

Lady Cunnington was only too happy to supervise.

When Elena accompanied Lord and Lady Cunnington to the newly renovated Olympic Theater just off Drury Lane, where they saw Mr. Emery in *Free and Easy*, the farce drew from her more laughter than she had uttered in months. She was so busy recalling the most amusing portions with her aunt and uncle during the intermissions that she did not notice the array of quizzing glasses raised in her direction from the pit and the boxes opposite.

They did not attend the buffet afterward, but went directly home. Settling to sleep that night, Elena recalled the evening's mirth with amazement. It was both cheering and disturbing to think she could have forgotten her grief over Rodney to such an extent.

The following morning Lady Cunnington said, "Elena, my dear, I am giving a musicale next Thursday. No more than three dozen people, as I detest crowds, but you enjoyed yourself so last night, I do believe you will feel up to the mark by then."

"I should think I would, Aunt Winifred," Elena said politely, though she quailed at her aunt's considering nearly forty people less than a crowd. "Shall I know anyone?"

"I doubt it. Your father and mother have been out of touch for so long. And of course you are at least two years past the normal time for being presented to the Queen."

Elena smiled a little. "A presentation isn't really considered necessary in the country, you know, Aunt."

"Ah, but it is in Town. You cannot get an invitation to Almack's or even to private soirees and routs unless you have attended one of her Majesty's drawing rooms. Anyway, it is all arranged."

"Oh, Aunt Winifred, must I? I own I care very little about routs and such. Besides, I *am* a widow, and it has been less than a year . . ."

"I have strict instructions to ignore that, my dear. The marriage was properly annulled. You are Miss Tyndale again, and . . ."

Suddenly Elena's good resolutions vanished. She rose abruptly from the table, her blue eyes afire. "I am *not* Miss Tyndale again and I don't wish to be! I cannot treat the past as though it never occurred. I loved Rodney. Can no one understand that? I loved him and I don't want to forget him!"

She ran from the room to the sound of her aunt's amazed "Indeed!" Fortunately, Lord Cunnington had already gone off to the City to consult with his solicitor, so no one else was present to observe her behavior save the two footmen, who never reacted to anything.

Elena was already ashamed of her outburst by the time Lady Cunnington followed her to the bedchamber she had been given on the second floor. Her impulsive tongue had betrayed her again, and she had no idea how her aunt would respond. She stood motionless and gazed out the window overlooking the terrace even after she became aware of Aunt Winifred's presence in the doorway, awaiting the expected dressing-down.

Finally it came. "You are being quite foolish, you know."

"Yes," Elena admitted, not turning from the window. It was far easier to agree to such pronouncements than to try to explain herself.

Lady Cunnington entered the room and closed the door behind her. "No matter what you considered it, nor how deeply you felt about Captain Farnsworth, you must remember that neither society nor your family has recognized the elopement as a true marriage. If you keep thinking of it as such and insist that others do, you will only become an object of pity and, I might add, of scorn. You must be thankful you have not been labeled a fallen woman for the simple reason that the Duke and Duchess have agreed to keep the matter quiet. Both legally and for your own good you are Miss Tyndale, unmarried daughter of a baronet and a very eligible young woman. A very attractive one, too, my dear, if you will allow me to say so."

Elena turned around in momentary outrage, hardly hearing the compliment. "But . . ."

"You must contrive to forget Captain Farnsworth." Although her eyes were sympathetic, Lady Cunnington's tone was steel.

"I have no wish to marry again."

"What is your alternative?"

Elena turned away from her aunt's pitying gaze, shrugging slightly.

"You have my sympathy," her aunt continued. "You also have my support, but only if you buck up, my girl, and do what is expected of you. No matter what your private feelings, we all have our duty, you know."

"Yes." Elena ran a finger across the spotless enameled windowsill until she touched the dark blue of the silk draperies. It occurred to her to say that marriage for the sake of duty alone appeared to be a dreary business indeed, but instead she said, "You're very good to me, Aunt Winifred. I hardly deserve it."

Her aunt came to her and laid an arm around her waist. "Nonsense. You have always been my favorite niece, and I am happy to be of service to your dear mother. But I must insist on your cooperation."

Elena turned and buried her face in Lady Cunnington's ample bosom. "You shall have it," she promised.

When Sir John had been forced to relinquish his position in the British embassy in Vienna, Elena was sixteen and still a schoolgirl. She spoke both German and French fluently, played the piano inaccurately but passionately, and had learned to dance the French quadrille and the German waltz as well as English and Scottish reels, though she had never attended a ball. Most of her life she had longed to do something significant and exciting. Instead, she studied history and geography with her strict German governess, copied the poetry of Dryden, Pope, and Shakespeare into her notebook with an increasingly elegant hand, and took long walks with her English nurse. Twice a week she endured tame little teas with other children of the British legation, most of whom were younger than she, after which they were allowed to play piquet or cribbage or fox-and-geese.

Whenever possible, she surreptitiously read her mother's romantic novels. From them she learned that no power on earth can separate two lovers who are fated for each other, and that when she found the one love of her life, she would live for him alone and care nothing for the world. This lesson seemed reinforced by the example of Lady Theresa herself, who had always put her husband before her daughter and was repaid by his complete devotion to both of them.

Since her mother had forbidden anyone to praise Elena's beauty to her face, and had assiduously guarded her from the admiration of men while in Vienna, Elena had returned to England quite unspoiled. She had discounted the occasional compliments of her maids, who were trained to that sort of thing, because, in her own imagination, her nose was not long enough to be attractively aristocratic and a small misplaced freckle below her left cheek spoiled forever her vision of a perfect alabaster complexion. Since she never gazed into her eyes in the mirror at times when they sparkled with mirth or grew soft with pity, she had no way of knowing how easily a man might lose himself in those dark-rimmed, luminous blue irises so heavily shadowed by black lashes.

She had been, therefore, both surprised and somewhat embarrassed when, even before her eighteenth birthday, several men in the neighborhood of Tyndale Green seemed to fall over themselves in the effort to attract her attention. Marriage proposals had even been made, but her parents had considered them premature. "You are much too young," Lady Theresa had warned Elena. "And besides, there are bigger and better fish."

Elena had not cared, for none of the men had really attracted her. They were either too old, or too wrapped up in themselves and their country pursuits, or too inarticulate to command more than passing interest. The cream of eligible bachelors, her mother had implied, would be in London. All Elena need do to capture one was to appear, and like a comet on the horizon, she would attract them all and be able to take her pick. Elena was not used to the idea that men should act so foolishly, and to deliberately attract them seemed shameless and even wicked. Now her loyalty to Rodney's memory inhibited her even further. She would attend whatever social functions her aunt wished, in return for Lady Cunnington's kindness, but she would encourage no man to address her. She had this thought firmly in mind when Lady Cunnington took her shopping the following day.

They drove in the phaeton, first to nearby Wigmore Street for another fitting by Lady Cunnington's dressmaker; then to Mr. Botibol's on Oxford Street for hat trimmings; and thence to the new glove and hosiery shop on Bond Street to lay in a supply of those essentials. Each time they left the carriage they were guarded fore and aft by two liveried footmen who opened doors, handed them down, and carried a growing armory of parcels. They were finally returning to Queen Anne Street in the open carriage, tired and eager for a lunch, when Elena was startled to see a man impeccably dressed in morning clothes, top hat, cane, and gray gloves, descending the stone steps of an imposing columned building. His lean face and arrogant chin, jutting over the swaths of white neckcloth and high starched collar, looked exactly like Lawrence MacLean. She dropped her eyes to her gloved hands and her heart beat faster.

"Why, I do believe that is the new Lord Harcourt," Lady Cunnington exclaimed, obviously looking in the same direction.

"Who is?"

"That young man who left Brooks's as we passed. He just came into his inheritance this past year. I'm surprised you didn't hear of it. Isn't Penton Hill in Huntingdonshire? I haven't seen him in half a dozen years, though I hear he has been out of the Army since last August. I wonder if he is still unmarried."

Elena remembered vaguely hearing of the death of the old Lord Harcourt. She recalled no mention of his successor. If it was indeed Lawrence MacLean, that explained his presence so near Tyndale Green, for Penton Hill, property of the Viscounts Harcourt, was only some six miles from it.

THE UNWELCOME SUITOR

The thought of his being in London, frequenting these very streets, was disturbing.

Miss Charlotte Saxton came to Lady Cunnington's musicale with her parents, Sir Guy and Lady Saxton. She was the first person Elena saw that evening who was of her own age. They had met the previous Sunday, when Elena had accompanied her aunt on a round of social calls.

Charlotte, a large-boned, hearty-mannered girl with a frank, open friendliness, had attended a finishing school the past two years, but her motions while walking through a drawing room still resembled those of a gangling colt. Yet once they had exchanged their mutual anxiety about the coming Queen's drawing room, Elena had quickly warmed to her as a fellow sufferer who was even less attuned than she to the milieu of London Society.

Though Charlotte's mother was petite and mannerly, Sir Guy Saxton, who much preferred the country with his racing horses and foxhounds, was as ill-at-ease at the musicale as a giant in a nursery. Elena suspected that the Saxtons had been invited only because Lady Cunnington perceived that a possible friendship between the two girls would take her niece out of herself.

"And who are the musicians to be?" Charlotte asked Elena as they companionably sipped a cup of punch. "My father declares he cannot abide any 'squalling females,' as he terms sopranos. I myself would much prefer a fiddler and some dancing."

"And I," Elena agreed with a smile. "However, my aunt says we haven't the room for dancing. But you and your father may rest easy. I've been told the only singer is a man, and he will do popular airs as well as opera. And then we'll hear a pianist from Germany who was supposed to have been a child prodigy like Mozart."

"How long ago?" Charlotte asked wryly, and Elena laughed.

Then Lady Cunnington separated them to take her niece around to meet the most important people. Elena was soon caught up in a welter of strange faces and names, ladies in high-waisted silks and muslins, fringes on their foreheads, and curls held in place by velvet ribbons or jeweled clasps; men in high collars, brocaded vests, and tight pantaloons. The ladies all wanted to know when Elena would be presented to her Majesty.

"The last week in May," Lady Winifred replied, "which certainly doesn't give us much time."

Elena was then flooded with advice from the women, some of whom inserted lurid stories concerning the mishaps of poor girls who had succumbed to nerves or heat during the long, tiring wait in line. Elena nodded and listened with growing dismay until she was rescued by the butler's announcement that the musicians were ready. Then they all proceeded upstairs to the music room.

There not being enough seats for everyone, the married men stood behind their spouses and the single ones, with permission, sprawled at the feet of a lady who had caught their fancy. In Elena's case the gentleman was Mr. Lionel Mountjoy, middle-aged bachelor son of a rich and prominent Tory, with a reputation as a dandy. Elena thought at first she liked Mr. Mountjoy, for, although he inclined to stoutness and suffered a receding hairline, his appearance was fastidious and his talk witty and informed. But as the evening progressed, she wished she could have taken back her permission for him to sit at her feet, for his effusive compliments began to

THE UNWELCOME SUITOR

put her to the blush. When he became so bold as to comment on her beautifully shod feet, she suddenly recalled a gruff voice asking, "Have you walking boots on?"

All at once Mr. Mountjoy's flattery dissolved in a fog of memory: her flushed outrage (had it been real?), those unusual flecked eyes and the way they had gazed at her, his rapid, determined stride through the woods, the impression he had given of strength and purpose. Lawrence MacLean—curt, mysteriously uncommunicative, intent only on performing a bloody necessity. She had thought she disliked him, was not now sure she did not. But the vivid image of him had become an inescapable part of her memory of her last day at home.

And so she mused through the concert while the celebrated Italian tenor, Tramezzani, poignantly interpreted arias from *Semele* and *Don Giovanni*, and the former piano prodigy, having established the seriousness of his art with several classical numbers, dazzled his audience by performing seventeen impromptu variations on the popular song, "Those Evening Bells." When he bowed at its end, everyone applauded with delight.

Avoiding Mr. Mountjoy's devoted gaze, Elena glanced toward the door as she clapped and found herself looking into the eyes of Lawrence MacLean, standing without, in the hall. He had apparently just arrived.

Supper awaited everyone in the reception room across the hall. As Elena rose, she was immediately besieged by Mr. Mountjoy and two other men for the privilege of taking her there. She was saved by her aunt, who interfered with a breezy smile and an authoritative "Come, Elena, my dear, here is someone you simply must meet." And so she came face to face again with Mr. Lawrence MacLean, who had, indeed, recently become the third Lord Harcourt.

She hadn't time to compose herself. When Lord Harcourt bowed in response to her aunt's introductions, she could only stammer. "How—how very odd, sir, that we should meet again here."

"If I may have the pleasure of escorting you to supper, I'll explain my presence most satisfactorily, Miss Tyndale," he offered, an unsettling gleam in his brown and saffron eyes.

"Then you two already know each other?" Lady Cunnington asked in amazement.

"I cannot say we know each other," Elena amended. "We have met, that is all, in very . . . very . . ."

"Unusual circumstances," Lord Harcourt supplied with a smile. "But all credit to you, Lady Cunnington, for providing us with a better opportunity for further acquaintance. Don't you agree, Miss Tyndale?"

"I . . ." Again she was left speechless. But when she looked away, she glimpsed Mr. Mountjoy nearby, awaiting his chance to claim her.

"I'd be pleased to go in to supper with you, Lord Harcourt," Elena said with what she hoped was the right combination of formality and courtesy, and smiled at her aunt, who beamed back at them before moving on to organize the rest of her guests.

3

She supposed she ate, as did everyone else, for the table was laden with various fresh fruits, with slices of cold meat and white and yellow cheeses, with lobster and crab morsels simmering in hot sauces, with biscuits and breads and tarts. Even so, she could not afterward recall tasting anything. There was abundant claret, which Elena barely touched because she was hardly aware of the long-stemmed goblet by her plate. Nor was she much aware of the three dozen ladies and gentlemen who crowded the long table decorated with flowers and candelabra, nor the six footmen who waited on them. She forgot to notice who Charlotte Saxton's supper partner was or what had happened to Mr. Mountjoy.

She was only aware of Lawrence MacLean, Viscount Harcourt, on her left. Reflecting halfway through the meal on her condition, she thought, My God, it was the same the evening I first met Rodney. She was amazed at her disgustingly erratic emotional state and began to avoid his gaze. The multitude of voices rising and falling about her seemed a flood threatening to drown her. She toyed with the food on her plate, no longer hearing him.

"May I ask what is troubling you, Miss Tyndale?"

Lord Harcourt's question, tinged with a harsh concern, finally penetrated. She made a valiant effort to clear her head and managed a faint smile. "Perhaps I am suffering from some sort of shock. I have rarely been at table in such numerous company. We have lived very quietly in the country, since my father is unwell. I—I am finding it difficult to take all this in."

He seemed to accept her little fiction with all seriousness. "I had a similar experience after returning from the Peninsula campaign. Nothing about ordinary social discourse seemed normal. I would find myself daydreaming in the midst of company, not hearing a word that was said to me."

"You are in the Army, Lord Harcourt?"

"Not any longer. I sold out about a year ago. My uncle was near death, and being his heir, I needed to return home and attend to numerous business transactions."

"A sad excuse, but I'm happy you will no longer need to face the prospect of enemy guns. Or did you enjoy war as so many men seem to do?"

He gave her a strange look. "No," he said abruptly. "There is nothing enjoyable about war."

"Yet you shoot exceedingly well. There must have been some satisfaction . . ."

"I never enjoy having to kill any living thing, be it horse or fox or Frenchman," he said. "Please believe me, madam." He said it with such emphasis that she immediately sought to reassure him.

"Certainly I believe you. Why should I not?"

"Good." He looked away and took a long drink of his wine. It seemed to be his turn to be troubled. She longed (disturbing symptom!) to know what made him so touchy and abrupt one minute, then perfectly polite the next. Instead, she turned to the gentleman on her right, whose presence she had largely neglected.

He, however, had already drunk too many glasses of wine, and did not respond to her question. When she returned her attention to Lord Harcourt, she caught him gazing at her in a bemused way.

Finally in control, she smiled inquiringly. "What have I done to be the object of such a look, Lord Harcourt?"

"I believe I have just remembered where I first saw you," he said.

"Before this past month?"

"Yes, long before. Last autumn, as a matter of fact. It was Cheltenham—the ball at the assembly rooms. You danced with Captain Farnsworth."

His staccato sentences dropped like fate on her heart. Her fork fell onto her plate with a little clatter. "Y-you knew . . . Captain Farnsworth?"

"I knew him well enough. We were both in the same regiment—the Scots Greys." The antagonism in his voice was clear.

"Oh!" Her soft exclamation sat between them like an invisible barrier to further speech. A hot rush of color lit her cheeks. She had to gulp, like a drowning person, for a good breath of air. With no thought save her extreme discomfort, she pushed back her chair.

"I beg your pardon," she mumbled, rose without a backward look, and left the room.

The balcony at the end of the hall overhung the veranda and looked down on the walled-in garden behind the house. In blind haste Elena walked through the French doors opening onto it. Her heart beating violently, she clutched the rail with both hands and stared, unseeing, down into the dark foliage, made mysterious by the play of light and shadow from the veranda's Japanese lanterns.

Her stomach churned and her mind whirled with apprehension. But before she could focus lucidly on her distress, she heard footsteps and then Lord Harcourt's voice say quietly, "There was a rumor that Farnsworth eloped that night with a girl of good family."

She caught her breath and clutched the rail harder.

"I don't remember seeing you again," he continued, "although I remained in Cheltenham for three more days."

"I . . . was taken ill that night," she said after a long pause. "I returned home early the next day. I had only recovered my health shortly before I met you near the fen."

"I'm delighted you have recovered, Miss Tyndale." His voice was correct, yet it held a certain caustic note and she wondered if he believed her. She whirled to face him, but he was in shadow, the light from the hall only silhouetting his figure.

"You knew about poor Farnsworth?" he asked.

"What . . . about him?"

"Only a few days later he was injured in a brawl in a tavern, and died soon afterward."

She made no pretense of surprise. "How did you know the manner of his death?"

"I was involved, unfortunately. You see . . ."

Even as he spoke, she knew, with awful clarity, who Lawrence MacLean, Lord Harcourt, was. "My God," she interrupted, "you killed him!"

His quick step forward alarmed her. Lantern light abruptly revealed his eyes and his startled expression seemed menacing and inscrutable. She sought to run past him into the house, but he caught her arm.

"Believe me, it was an accident," he said urgently.

She froze. "Kindly let me pass, Lord Harcourt." Her voice was as icy as her limbs.

After an endless moment he released his grip without a word and stood aside. Her posture carefully correct, she walked the length of the hall, then turned to the stairway. Once she knew his eyes could no longer follow her, she gathered her flimsy skirts and ran to the sanctuary of her bedchamber.

At breakfast the next morning Lady Cunnington tried patiently to find out why Elena had departed the table so hastily the previous evening and, especially, why she had failed to return to bid their guests good night.

"I'm sorry, Aunt Winifred," Elena mumbled, "I can't explain."

"Can't explain!" Lady Cunnington echoed in disbelief. "Come, come, my girl, this won't answer. I'm here to help you, you know. And I thought you and Lord Harcourt were doing splendidly."

Elena only shook her head. The footman brought her a steaming pot of tea and a plate with two hot muffins. He poured a cup and proffered milk and sugar. Elena took both without thinking, though she ordinarily did not use sugar.

"He followed you after you left the table," Lady Cunnington pursued. "Did you speak with him then?"

"Yes. I told him to leave me alone."

"Did you! Was he importunate, then? I would say that is quite unlike him, unless he has altered marvelously in the last few years."

"I do not like him."

"He has asked if he may call on you."

Elena looked up from the muffin she was buttering, startled. "I hope, dear Aunt, that you said no."

"Why on earth should I? He is eminently suitable, a gentleman, a lord, and at least comfortably well off. Perhaps even rich, once the estate matters have been settled. He is also very attractive, is he not?"

"I do not find him so."

"Well, perhaps you will change your mind. As a matter of fact, Elena dear, he is not the only one whose attention you captured. Several other gentlemen asked the same. I expect I shall have to establish an 'at home' to accommodate all your beaux. Once the presentation is over, of course."

Elena heard her with mixed emotions. The idea of holding court for a group of male admirers filled her with dismay, but if she could lose Lawrence MacLean in the crowd, if she pointedly ignored him, he might become discouraged.

With a sudden smile she turned to her aunt. "That is most kind of you, Aunt Winifred."

Lady Cunnington said briskly, "That's more like, child. You really do feel better? Would you like an egg?"

"I have quite enough to eat."

"You shall need your strength, you know. We must begin planning your presentation in earnest. The Queen's drawing room is not far off. My dressmaker is coming at noon with some designs for you to choose from. It is ridiculous, I know, but you must learn to handle not only a train but a hoop. And feathers in your hair."

"Feathers, truly? I have always disliked the fashion. And how does one keep them attached?"

"I should rather have called them plumes. They

THE UNWELCOME SUITOR

are attached to a cap or a bandeau, of course, as is the train." She smiled benignly, certain she had caught Elena's interest.

Elena, vaguely dismayed, returned to her tea, drank it too hastily, and burned her tongue.

4

Two days after Lady Cunnington's evening musicale Lawrence MacLean (which name he still preferred, at least to himself) quarreled with his mother and canceled an engagement with a young lady, thereby violating two of his most cherished precepts.

All because he was unable to think of anyone or anything beyond Miss Elena Tyndale. The look in her eyes when she uttered those fatal words, "You killed him!" in such a shocked undertone had left him nearly sleepless for two nights.

He had realized that Elena had been Farnsworth's runaway bride as soon as he placed her as the Captain's dancing partner last September in Cheltenham. He had seen her face that night as they waltzed past him—the face of a woman in love. He had thought, with disgust, That bastard Farnsworth, how easily he wins them over. The poor girl should be warned. Watching them the rest of the dance, he had toyed with the prospect of doing just that, but he really had no right to interfere. He didn't even know the girl, and it would only cause further trouble with Farnsworth, of which he had had enough.

Yet the girl was so lovely, with her flushed cheeks and vivid coloring and her rapt face, that he could not keep his eyes off her and was more than once tempted, unpolitic though it might be, to approach her once the dance was over.

Then an acquaintance had engaged him in conversation and later on he could find neither the girl nor the Captain.

He had seen her only from a distance, in profile, in motion. He had never stood directly before her, taking in the effect of those fathomless blue eyes, nor seen the uptilted corner of her lovely mouth when she smiled. That fact—and the angry mood he had been in when faced with the necessity of shooting his favorite hunter—must have been why he had not recognized her on their chance encounter in Huntingdonshire. The resemblance had come to him only at Lady Cunnington's supper table, in a flash, when she lifted her eyes to respond to his question as to what troubled her. It had been there again—that rapt look which, this time, actually seemed to be directed toward him. It had been brief, quickly veiled, but his heart had turned over. As had happened near the fen, he had found himself being abrupt and unpleasant, just to cover the sensation.

And then, what had he done but pursue the connection, like a sapskull, thereby confirming the date of his first sight of her, and that had led, inevitably, to the confrontation on the balcony.

You killed him.

His quick defensive response had not penetrated her horror. He had realized almost immediately that she was not ready to hear his explanation, even if he had been able to force her to stay and listen to it, so he had let her go. Perhaps that had been a mistake. For the longer he waited to tell her the truth, the more ingrained would be her belief that he had been responsible for Farnsworth's death.

Which, in a way, he was. Thinking the whole thing over, he began to doubt he could ever satisfactorily explain himself to her, even if he could convince her he had not actually struck the final blow. For he could not deny that the fight had taken place, nor that his own words had instigated it.

It had all come about so unexpectedly: two former fellow officers meeting at an isolated, rainswept inn on the Yorkshire moors, the only customers in the taproom. The situation had demanded an assumed friendliness in spite of past friction between them. They had hailed each other in surprise and shared a table and a bottle of porter. Lawrence, his wet cloak and boots steaming before the open fireplace and his bones finally warmed, had relaxed enough to recall old times in the Army in Portugal, where Captain Farnsworth had acquired a reputation for loving and leaving dark-eyed *senhoritas*. Lawrence, on the other hand, having been jilted by a pretty, shallow young lady in Portsmouth during his early Army days, had been wary of women then and took plenty of chaff about his apparent disinterest, even in those of "easy virtue." Farnsworth had been one of the worst, mocking Lawrence's "purity" and "tenderheartedness," and taking a certain satisfaction in his own reputation as a ladies' man. So Lawrence was surprised when his good-humored attempt to tease Farnsworth about those days elicited a quick "That's all over now." A glance toward the ceiling had given him away.

"You're with a woman now?" Lawrence had guessed. Then, after a pause he asked, "What ever happened to the lovely lady I saw you with at Cheltenham?"

He recalled only too vividly the satisfied smile on Farnsworth's face. "That *is* the one I'm with,

THE UNWELCOME SUITOR

MacLean. Did you think it another barmaid? No, those days are over forever. We were married in Scotland five days ago."

The declaration abruptly halted Lawrence's attempt at lighthearted banter. "A lady has run away with you to Gretna Green?"

Farnsworth had responded to his change of mood with a defensive truculence. "Yes. What of it?"

"What of it? What about the woman you married in Portugal?"

"I married no one in Portugal!"

All the old antagonism rose, like bile, in Lawrence's throat. "It won't fadge, Farnsworth! I remember only too well. Our mutual friend, Daniels, attended as your witness, or were you too half-sprung to remember? My God, I knew you were a rabshackle, but I'd have thought bigamy was beneath even *your* style."

Farnsworth leapt to his feet, his jaw tight, his eyes flashing. "That's a lie, you interfering bastard!"

His display of temper turned Lawrence perversely calm. He leaned back in his chair and drawled, "Ah, how quickly we forget when it comes to a woman, eh, *capitaõ de amor?*"

"I should have finished you off in Spain when I had the opportunity."

"You're calling me out again? How charming. But I don't see your weapon tonight—"

He had not finished his sentence when Farnsworth, ignoring liquor glasses and bottles, leapt over the table and grabbed Lawrence by the throat. The chair broke as they fell to the muddy floor, but Farnsworth's grip on his Adam's apple remained, as singleminded as a mad dog's.

Finally Lawrence managed a knee in Farnsworth's abdomen, threw him off, and when they had both lurched to their feet, planted a blow on his jaw. Farnsworth reeled sideways toward the big hearth, struck his head against the rough stone mantel, then slumped forward against the sharp edge of the brass fender, cutting his eye and knocking himself unconscious.

Lawrence had gone for a surgeon and, later, paid for the damage done to glassware and furniture. But he had not had the courage, that night, to reenter the inn to confront the girl who had danced with Farnsworth and been so obviously in love little more than a week before. Even though he had not known, then, that Farnsworth had died, he could not face her and say, "I did it. I'm responsible for your lover's battered, bloody face..."

He should have, he realized now. He ought to have returned with the surgeon and seen the episode through to the end, tried to explain, offered his services in anyway possible. Yet surely she would have spurned him as completely then as now, for he *had* killed Farnsworth, by unguarded words, by the blow that had sent the man careening toward the fireplace. Could she ever understand or forgive that when he had not quite forgiven himself?

He remembered her quick retreat at the mention of Farnsworth's name. He had been appalled then to realize her identity. He should have left immediately, gone out of her life quietly and with good grace. To follow her and insist on the connection, with his idiotic need to know the truth, had undone him. For in the same moment that she had uttered her icy accusation, he had realized he loved her.

So there it was—he was in love. As he had hoped never to be again. As he had been warned, by a wise and generous woman, that he would be, someday. Love—unwanted, illogical, overpowering as ever.

THE UNWELCOME SUITOR 43

Stronger than his common sense. Stronger, he hoped, then her mistrust and aversion, which he was determined to overcome.

Acting on the determination, he paid a visit to Queen Anne Street the very next day, but she would not receive him. He drew some encouragement, however, from Lady Cunnington, who sent back a note by a footman, though she didn't see him herself. "Miss Tyndale and I will be taking the air in the park, about 5 o'clock Sunday afternoon, provided the weather holds fair."

A clear invitation to encounter them there and exchange a few words. Even such a limited meeting was better than nothing and might provide an opening. It did, however, require that he alter previous plans and that led to the quarrel with his mother, which, given the circumstances and both their natures, was inevitable.

For as long as Lawrence could remember, his sharp-faced, diminutive mother, Alice MacLean, had delighted in dominating everyone about her. His sister, Lizbeth, had married her Scottish laird before she ever had a London Season, so anxious had she been to get away from her mother's stranglehold. Lawrence had sometimes wondered if his father had not deliberately succumbed to heart failure in order to escape his wife's domineering ways. His younger brother Lambert's rebellion came out in other ways. While appearing to be a sunny, pliable boy, he was given to occasional crude practical jokes which were forever getting him into trouble. But then, Mrs. MacLean had always been more lenient with Lambert, her youngest. For her first son, Lawrence, she usually marshaled all her resources.

Being equally strong-minded, Lawrence had tried not to allow it without open rebellion or rudeness.

When she had taken rooms in Cambridge the first winter of his studies there, thinking to oversee his activities, he had left the university and joined the Army. Even now, after his years spent fighting the French and in spite of his refusal to live in the same house with her (he had taken a flat on Clarges Street, but it was still much too close to his mother's house in Albemarle Street), she was forever sending him little notes by the servants, trying to plan his social life for him. Though he rarely acceded to these demands, his conscience still required that he take tea with her once a week.

This Saturday afternoon he used the ritual as an opportunity to challenge her long-standing assumption that he would someday marry his second cousin, Lady Cordelia Radcliffe, who had lived with his mother ever since her parents had died seven years before. He had hoped to work into the subject casually, as Mrs. MacLean ranted on about how Cordelia had looked forward to seeing more of him this summer in London, but finally he simply interrupted her.

"Mother, I know your hopes in the matter, but I must make it clear to you that I do not intend to marry Cordelia."

Mrs. MacLean, her train of thought broken, only stared at him as though he spoke Arabic. The silence grew awkward.

"And so," he continued at last, looking down at the tea she had just poured for him, "you must hold me excused from escorting the two of you to evensong tomorrow."

"Really, Lawrence! What does going to church have to do with it?"

"Well, to begin with, I have other plans for the

THE UNWELCOME SUITOR

afternoon. But besides that . . . Mother, you simply must stop creating these little occasions for me to be with her. It won't do. I don't want her to continue with false hopes."

Mrs. MacLean sighed and her prominent jaw appeared to relax in defeat—a deceptive sign. "Now, Lawrence, what sort of nonsense is that? Don't you realize Cordelia has doted on you ever since you went to the Army?"

"Mother, you can't mean that. Cordelia was only twelve when I went to the Army."

"Nevertheless, she has always loved you. I'll admit I encouraged her in it, but only because I believed you would do your duty eventually. The two of you are so suited." Her voice had become fervent.

"In what way?"

"In every way, of course. She has been part of the family for years." Mrs. MacLean's brown eyes grew penetrating as she pretended to sip tea. Lawrence only held his, a little awkwardly, forgetting about it. "What made you change your mind?"

"I haven't changed it. I have only just decided I must face the issue and make things clear to you."

"But why now?"

He said, as coolly as possible, "I've met someone else." (What a lackluster way to put this sudden, engulfing emotion!)

"Someone else!" Mrs. MacLean repeated in astonishment. "Someone *else?* Who is she?"

"I-it may come to nothing. I would rather not say, just yet. But . . ."

"Then why this need to burn your bridges, so to speak, when nothing has hap—"

"Mother, I am not . . . I have never broached the subject of marriage to Cordelia. It has all been in your minds—the two of you. I am simply telling you you must forget it, once and for all. I will never marry her."

"How could you be so heartless?" She had met every hesitant sentence with admirable restraint. Now she realized he meant it, and her indignation overflowed. Without pause she embarked, with numerous embellishments, on the theme of his failure to act responsibly as the eldest son, the new Viscount Harcourt who would someday, she was sure, be a power in the government. From there she returned to his terrible unfairness to his mother and that dear, sweet child he had always seemed so fond of. He bore it as long as he could, then rose and planted a kiss on her rouged cheek.

"I'm truly sorry that I cannot please you in this, Mother, but it's no use your going on about it. And if you'll kindly give my regrets to Cordelia concerning tomorrow . . ."

She turned her face away. "You shall do that yourself. I believe she is in her sitting room, awaiting a word from you. And I hope you will be able to live with yourself, once you have destroyed all her hopes."

Fortunately Lady Cordelia herself was not so emotional. Their conversation was short and quite ordinary. During it Lawrence thought to himself that, yes, she was sweet and even pretty at times, but she had so little life in her, so little enthusiasm. Surely he could not have been expected to know she "doted on him," as his mother insisted.

At last he remarked, "I'm sorry, Delia, but I will be unable to escort you and Mother to evensong tomorrow."

She looked up from her everlasting needlework (she had not bothered to give him more than a brief glance when he first entered) and said that it was quite all right, a footman could accompany them. Her lips did not smile and her eyes did not question him. He felt only relief when he left her presence.

Sunday afternoon in May had never been prettier. The pastoral greenery of Hyde Park perfectly set off the ladies who rode in open *vis-à-vis* or phaetons driven by solemn coachmen in powdered wigs and bright livery. Lace-trimmed parasols and plumed hats fluttered in the breeze. Precious stones at brow, neck, and wrist flashed in the sunlight. But it was the alluring sidelong glances of the ladies themselves that attracted the gazes of the mounted gentlemen in their starched white cravats and brass-buttoned coats, leather breeches, and polished topboots. The grazing cattle and sheep scattered about the grounds barely heeded this human pageant, being quite used to it.

Lawrence rode his Arabian gray, Starlight, along Rotten Row, across the Serpentine, and back through the trees toward Hyde Park Corner, counter to the flow of carriages, lifting his hat and bowing from the saddle to those he recognized but seeking only one face.

At last he saw Lady Cunnington's blue-and-ivory-liveried coachman driving the baroness's phaeton, her coat of arms gleaming on each polished cherry-wood side panel. His heart did a strange little dance as he recognized Lady Cunnington herself, handsome and formidable in green, nearly obstructing his view of her niece. Elena was adorable in yellow, with white lace about her throat and wrist and black ringlets framing her face under her wide-brimmed yellow hat.

He doffed his top hat easily enough but had to

clear his throat before his first "Good afternoon, ladies," could be heard.

"What a fine day it is, indeed," Lady Cunnington returned cordially while Elena merely acknowledged his greeting with a nod. "Pray, Lord Harcourt, ride with us so we may talk. I've been meaning to ask you about your dear mother."

A flush grew unmistakably on Elena's face and she looked away. Lawrence wheeled his horse around and settled it to match the gait of the phaeton's pair. "Mother is well, thank you, Lady Cunnington," he returned.

"She is in London now, I believe? I must call on her. And your sister and brother, are they with her as well?"

"Lizbeth has remained in Edinburgh with her husband this year. Lambert is at Eton still, in fifth form." He hoped he did not speak impatiently. He could hardly frame his answers, ordinary though they were, while trying to think of some way to draw Elena into the conversation. To make it more awkward she was on the far side of the carriage, a situation he could not correct without rudeness.

But now, at the mention of his siblings, Elena glanced toward him with a hint of interest in her violet eyes. He inclined his head toward her, trying to hold her attention. "Have you ridden often in the park, Miss Tyndale, since your arrival in London?" (Bird-witted question! Where was his ingenuity, his wit?)

"This is the first time, Lord Harcourt," she admitted stiffly, as though she must force the words out. Her glance dropped immediately to her lap.

"And are you enjoying it?" he pursued.

She looked up then and smiled, and an unexpected dimple at the edge of her mouth turned her expression roguish. "I should prefer a good canter, sir, riding on the horse, not behind it. Men are so fortunate."

He smiled back. "Not always. And I'm sure your wish can be realized. But not here, nor at this time of day."

"Heaven forbid," Lady Cunnington put in decisively. "We should all get in the most terrible tangle, going at such a clip, and what would be the point?"

Lawrence laughed outright at the image she had conjured up. Apparently offended, Lady Cunnington nodded a good-day and, before he had time to frame a response, told her coachman to drive home. The horses were pulled out of line and put to a trot, and he was left behind.

5

Elena awoke Monday morning with a headache and Lady Cunnington insisted she return to bed after breakfast. Then, after seeing that she was well dosed with calomel pills and comfortably ensconced in dressing gown and slippers on the chaise longue under a comforter, her aunt left the house on a shopping expedition.

Elena was still sitting there with Jane hovering nearby in case she wanted anything, idly leafing through the latest copy of *La Belle Assemblée* and feeling slightly ashamed of the importance Aunt Winifred gave a simple headache, when a footman came to the door with a card on a salver. Jane took it and brought it to her mistress, who picked it up with surprise. When she read "Lawrence MacLean, Viscount Harcourt," she dropped it onto the silver dish as though it had burned her.

"He's here, Jane? Ask Ross what he wants."

Jane returned to the door and allowed the footman in. "His Lordship has asked to see you, miss," Ross explained.

"You may say I am indisposed and can receive no one." As the footman turned to carry out her wishes, Elena added, "No, wait. Say that . . . I am not at home to him. Nor shall I be at any time in the future, should he presume to call."

Ross only said, "Yes, ma'am," with no more than a flicker of the eye, but Jane drew in her breath with suppressed disapproval. At that point Elena's headache, which had nearly disappeared, began to throb again and she sent Jane to ask for a pot of tea.

She had first experienced the headache the day before in the park, when Lord Harcourt had unexpectedly appeared again. She was quite sure such a reaction to his presence was all due to knowing he had been the instrument of Rodney's death.

How can he? she wondered over and over. How can he persist in these attentions to me? He surely has guessed I'm the one who married Captain Farnsworth. He must know how it affects me to meet my husband's murderer. How can he be so unfeeling?

Other uncomfortable thoughts intruded, converting her headache into a throbbing omnipresent monster. Her mother had assured her that only they and the Malverns knew of her elopement, yet Lord Harcourt said there had been rumors. What rumors? Had she been identified as the woman involved in the elopement or was he the only one who had guessed? But if he had seen her dance with Rodney at the assembly rooms and put two and two together, others might have done the same. The only saving factor was that she had not been well known —people were constantly confusing her connection to the Duke and Duchess of Malvern, thinking her a relative instead of the daughter of a friend.

But if others had identified her as that woman, she would be labeled either deceitful or, in her aunt's phrase, a fallen woman. Her mother, eager to see her properly married, had cheerfully brushed aside such considerations. Not for the first time Elena thought that her mother was simply eager to have her out of the household, to have Sir John to herself. If only she had resisted the idea more... But would it have done any good? If only she had not come to London, had never encountered Lawrence MacLean with his fascinating, changeable eyes and his forceful, abrupt presence and his fortune and title, which made him so welcome in London's best drawing rooms. She could refuse to receive him at home, but how could she avoid him once she had been presented to the Queen and must accept all those unwelcome invitations Aunt Winifred anticipated?

By late morning Elena, recognizing the folly of lying in her room and allowing her worries to prey on her mind, arose despite the headache and announced she would have a bath, and Jane must lay out her new blue muslin and the matching ribbons for her hair. By the time Lady Cunnington returned home, she insisted she was once more feeling fine. When Charlotte Saxton and her mother arrived for a late lunch, it was almost true, and she had succeeded in pushing thoughts of Lord Harcourt to the back of her mind.

During a meal of turtle soup, biscuits, and baked salmon, Charlotte, Lady Saxton, Elena, and Lady Cunnington talked about the coming Presentation. The Queen, who received the new crop of debutantes each May, was getting old and her eyes dim, but this did not in the least excuse any oversight in dress and deportment. It addition to various hawk-eyed members of the Court, the Prince Regent himself might be present. Even if he were not (for the Prince preferred diversions with his favorites at Brighton or Carleton House to watching a tedious procession of young girls dipping curtsies and not quite kissing the back of his mother's hand), the word got back to him if a girl was pretty enough, and she was invited to a levee at Carleton House later in the summer.

"Well, if beauty is the criterion, it won't be me," Charlotte said with resignation. "But I don't really mind, I guess. No matter how splendidly he dresses, the Prince Regent is fat and no longer young, and I needn't go to Carleton House to meet the people who matter."

"What other people matter to you?" Elena asked mischievously. "Have you picked out your future husband so soon?"

Charlotte glanced to her mother, who was discussing the exorbitant cost of London's private dancing and deportment masters (whose instruction her daughter still sadly needed) with Lady Cunnington. "Have you noticed Mr. Stuart Jaeger?" she asked in a stage whisper. "He is a fine-looking man—not handsome, but well set up. And definitely not a dandy, but I detest dandies. He's straightforward and honest. We were dinner partners and we talked about his study of waterfowl. But I'm afraid I was too taken with him to seem anything but dim-witted."

"Oh, then he was at the musicale?"

"You didn't notice him," Charlotte reproached her. "But perhaps that's just as well. Any man you set your cap at would never look at me twice."

Elena laughed away the jealousy she heard in Charlotte's voice. "What fudge! You needn't worry, anyway. I don't intend to set my cap at anyone."

Charlotte was amazed. "Does Lady Cunnington know that? After all, that's why all this fuss with wardrobe and presentations and routs—to find a husband."

"Oh, but . . ." Elena paused, flustered for a moment. "All I meant was, I shall probably not fall in love."

She could see that her response was about to provoke further questions, but Lady Saxton saved her by saying in a loud voice, "Well, Charlotte, we really must be on our way. It was a perfectly charming luncheon, my dear Baroness, and so delightful to be able to talk to you *tête-à-tetê* this way." She rose, signaling Charlotte to follow suit.

"You are quite well?" Lady Cunnington asked Elena as they returned to the reception room after the Saxtons' departure. "Your headache has left you?"

"Yes, thank you, Aunt."

"I'm so glad." Then she frowned and motioned Elena to sit beside her on a sofa. "But what is this I hear about your not only refusing to see Lord Harcourt but, in effect, cutting him dead?"

Elena's eyes dropped to her lap to hide her anger. Ross had evidently repeated to his mistress everything that had transpired in her absence. "He has quite hounded me and I want him to understand clearly that I don't wish to see him again."

"Hounded you? Nonsense! How could he have, just by speaking to us in the park for a few moments yesterday? I don't understand you at all, child!"

"I'm sorry, Aunt, I—I have just developed a-an antipathy to him. I can't help it." She jumped up from her seat. "Do you suppose I could go for a walk?"

Lady Cunnington looked up at her, still frowning. "Well, I cannot join you now. I have some correspondence to attend to and then I simply must have a lie-down before tea."

"Could I take Jane, then, to accompany me?"

"That would do, I suppose. So long as you don't go far. Just around Cavendish Square, I should think. And don't forget your parasol."

Impulsively Elena bent and kissed her, surprising them both. "Thank you! A little exercise is what I really need."

"As for Lord Harcourt," her aunt reminded Elena, as she was about to dance out of the room, "his mother and I were at school together—not that we got on, particularly—but I've followed her son's career with some interest, and I doubt you could do better."

Elena stopped and pressed her hands to her head in sudden distress. "No, dear Aunt, no! You mustn't push him on me or—or I shall be forced to return to Tyndale Green!"

Before Lady Cunnington could reprove her again, she had vanished.

Jane had served Elena for about half a year. A country girl from near Buckden, she had begun in the Tyndale establishment at the age of eighteen, four years before. Thanks to her instinct for neatness, a willingness to do more than she was asked, and a sober disposition, she had quickly progressed from kitchen maid to parlor maid, then to upstairs maid, and finally to Elena's personal maid. Elena thought that Jane, whose approval or disapproval of her mistress's actions always showed on her round face, was born to be a chaperone. Lady Theresa had surely recognized this quality when she had appointed the girl to her present post shortly after the violent ending to Elena's elopement, as though hoping Jane's sober presence would prevent a repetition of such behavior.

Jane, carrying her mistress's reticule, remained

slightly behind Elena as they walked around the circular perimeter of Cavendish Square. The day was cloudy and chill, promising rain, and Elena wore her new lavender poplin pelisse with braid down the front and around the hem. Her small white-plumed velvet hat, also lavender, was protected by a matching lavender parasol, which, if subject to a real downpour, would be well-nigh useless.

Because Elena knew Jane disapproved her present course regarding Lord Harcourt, their progress was a silent one. Elena walked briskly once around the circle, then began a repetition of the route. "It might come on for rain soon, Miss Elena," Jane objected.

"It may, indeed, but I propose we continue our exercise until it does. There are worse things than a little damp clothing," Elena returned. Still she walked faster, and missed seeing a man turn in their direction at the corner of Henrietta Place.

Several paces farther on, she was surprised at what seemed to be Jane's attempt to move abreast of her. She turned sharply and met the amused gaze of Lord Harcourt.

With an exclamation of alarm, she glanced back at her maid, but Jane, apparently deliberately, had fallen several feet behind them.

"It's quite all right," Lawrence MacLean said, making so bold as to steer her elbow forward with his gloved hand. "Your girl will keep an eagle eye on us and make sure I do nothing to offend you."

"Your presence offends me quite enough, Viscount," Elena retorted. She refused to look at him after the first moment's recognition and walked even more swiftly. "Why won't you leave me alone?"

"Because I must find out why you have refused to see me. What have I done?"

"You know perfectly well."

"I don't. I swear it."

She turned away, biting her lip, thinking to freeze him out with silence. But the strain of his presence was too much. Finally she said stiffly, "You were responsible for Captain Farnsworth's death. And if you have not already guessed, he was my husband." (Surely, knowing that, he would desist!)

"I had guessed. And I am sorry for it—more sorry than I can tell you. But his death was an accident."

"You were fighting him, were you not?"

"I defended myself, that is all. I was exonerated of blame in the investigation."

She could not avoid a quick startled glance at him. "I didn't know . . . of any investigation."

"No. Because you fled home and were insulated from any further references to the episode."

"I know, it was cowardly of me," Elena said bitterly.

"Not at all. But you must admit you have come to your own conclusions without proof."

She shook her head, but her footsteps slowed as she considered her statement. "Even so, you must have been his enemy. I realize now it was your name he spoke in such anger with his dying breath." She paused, waiting for a response, but he gave none. "So . . . don't you see?" she pleaded. "I cannot accept your—your friendship. The wound is not healed. Your very presence is a reminder of what happened to him."

"But if I am not allowed to see you, how can I change your mind?"

She stopped to face him. "Just leave me alone! There are any number of other young ladies . . ."

"No, there are none but you," he interrupted fiercely. "I am blind to all others, now I have met you."

She caught her breath and her hand flew to her mouth. "Oh, you mustn't . . ."

"Come," he said. "Walk on. Your maid is staring at us."

Reluctantly she moved on, though she knew Jane would remain at a discreet distance whatever her own pace. Her face was suddenly hot in spite of the day's chill, her heart was not behaving at all, and her legs felt almost too weak to bear her weight.

"You don't really despise me," he said, watching her closely, his hand once more discreetly supporting her elbow.

"W-whether I do or not isn't to the point, Viscount . . ."

"Lawrence," he interrupted.

She threw him a glance, a mute plea for mercy. "I mean . . . that doesn't signify. I can't return your attentions. Nor any man's. Not now."

"I thought you had come to London to catch a husband."

"You have a horrid way of putting it, Lord Harcourt! It was my family's idea, not mine."

He was silent a long while and she dared steal a glance at him. His lean-jawed face was softened in thought. He turned to her and caught her gaze. "Of course," he murmured. "Forgive me." She looked away, trembling again. "But you cannot mourn forever," he added.

"Everyone tells me that," she agreed tartly. "I am quite sick of it."

"Captain Farnsworth was only a man, not a god."

"You have no right to even speak of him."

"Haven't you ever wondered why he was in such a hurry to marry you?"

"What are you insinuating, sir?"

THE UNWELCOME SUITOR

"That perhaps you didn't know him as well as you ought to have done."

She drew in an angry breath. "Oh, you are despicable, you are past bearing! How dare you suggest such things?"

She had stopped again to face him, too aggrieved to realize what she did.

His amber-shot brown eyes seemed to darken as he returned her gaze. "I imagine I shall dare almost anything," he said at last, "to make you mine."

She could only stare at him, speechless.

The hint of a smile played on his lips, then was gone. His gaze held hers, mesmerizing her, sending chill after chill through her. "At least you are not indifferent to me," he observed. "I'll take my leave now, Elena, my love." He raised his hand to stop her outraged response. "Oh, yes, you are my love, whether you acknowledge it or no. And I beg your pardon, but I never delivered the message I came round with this morning. Would you care to ride with me in the park tomorrow morning—on the back of a horse, not in a carriage?"

"I cannot," she said, breathless from the impact of his words.

"Some other time, then?"

"Are you quite deaf? I don't wish to see you ever again."

He only smiled, bowed again, lifted his hat to her, and was gone.

Elena looked about her as though she were coming out of a daze. They were, thank God, on the corner of Harley Street, only a few paces from home. She was suddenly very cold and trembling, and she reached a hand to Jane's arm to steady herself. "Could he have meant that, do you think?" she asked.

"Meant what, mum?" Jane asked. Her glance was bright with pity.

Elena shook her head. "I . . . Never mind." She began walking up Harley Street. "Let's hurry, it's starting to rain." After a minute she added, "Why did you desert me in such a fashion, Jane?"

"Desert you? Oh, no, mum! 'Is Lordship's a good man. 'E deserves a chance."

Elena flung her a suspicious look. "You are *all* conspiring against me."

"Beggin' your pardon, mum, but I'm fer you if anyone is," Jane said firmly. "An' I say any lady'd be a fool to pass over such a one."

"Stop!" Elena commanded. "You have said quite enough."

And yet, and yet . . . She hastened her steps toward the Cunnington mansion while the occasional sprinkles became a steady mist. Too deep in thought to notice the weather, she was trying to suppress the frightening notion that Jane was right.

6

The following week fittings for the Court gown took precedence over everything else. Elena was amazed at how complicated a creation it was. A net and lace overskirt, dipping low in front and back, was to be caught up at the sides with yellow rosebuds. Under it, more white net embroidered with rows of half-moons, horizontal trellises of flowers, and loops of gold braid would hang over a white satin underskirt edged in scalloped lace. All must hang perfectly across the hoop from the frilled bodice, which, thanks to fashion's high waist and decolletage, seemed comparatively inconsequential.

On her head would be a cap of white satin adorned with gold lace which secured both the plumes floating about her head and the train that fell across the back of the gown to the floor. Earrings and necklace of pearls, white satin slippers with designs in seed pearls, elbow-length white gloves, and a gold filigreed fan completed the ensemble. The hairdresser practiced twice on her, hemming and hawing, trying to find the best way to show Elena's long, lustrous black hair to advantage under a headdress that seemed designed to make hair superfluous. Elena had refused to follow fashion and have it cut and curled except the the part that framed her face.

The rehearsals during the final week only accelerated the frantic pace toward the Queen's drawing room, which was to take place on Thursday afternoon. Elena and Charlotte practiced together as Lady Cunnington posed as the Queen at the end of the reception room. Both girls, wearing the unaccustomed hoop and with a long piece of muslin pinned in place for the train, practiced walking, turning, carrying the train over one arm, then dropping it for a footman to arrange behind them. Over and over they went through the ritual, accompanied by instructions and warnings from Aunt Winifred.

The curtsy must be graceful and sweeping, and heaven help the poor girl who lost her balance or whose heel got caught in hem or train. If the Queen proffered her cheek, one kissed it lightly (with *dry* lips); if she proffered only her hand, one must take it and not quite kiss the back of it. The privilege of kissing the royal cheek was usually reserved for the daughters of the Court or people well known to the Sovereign (at which Charlotte and Elena drew sighs of relief), but could be extended to any girl the Queen took a fancy to on sight. They would do well to be prepared for the unexpected favor, since a momentary lack of *savoir faire* could be a source of keen embarrassment.

One did not speak to the Queen unless spoken to, and then one's tones must be audible but not loud and, of course, cultured and appropriate. Finally, one must back away rather than turn away, and not become entangled in one's train, at the same time preparing to bow before other royalty that might be present.

During rehearsals Elena managed to keep her mind on the business at hand, but fittings for the dress, at which she was treated as a prize doll by both the dressmaker and Lady Cunnington, often found her staring into a corner, mentally miles away. She had not seen Lord Harcourt since the encounter in Cavendish Square. He did not again visit the house on Queen Anne Street or ride in Hyde Park. She had thought this was what she wanted—freedom from his presence. Instead, she only wondered each time she went out if she might see him and was vaguely disappointed when she did not.

For days the remembrance of his declaration continued to disturb her. His boldness had been incredible and she kept telling herself she was rightfully offended. And yet . . .

One night she dreamed again of Rodney. Not the nightmare of his death, which had previously haunted her, but embarrassingly enough, dreams of the activities of the marriage bed.

For the short time she had experienced it, Rodney's lovemaking had amazed and disturbed her. Totally ignorant of what to expect, she had found it hard to believe that such intimacy—the nakedness, the exploration of the secrets of her body—was a proper part of marriage. Timidly she had begun to realize that she might, eventually, enjoy it, but she doubted she would ever find it as profoundly liberating as Rodney apparently did. But the dream told her otherwise, told her that she would not only welcome but crave such intimacy. In her fantasy all her inhibitions fell away and she offered herself eagerly. Even when the face of Rodney, leaning over her, somehow changed to that of Lawrence MacLean . . .

Stirring from sleep, she was trembling and on fire. Only after she had truly awakened did she manage to work up a healthy disgust at the dream, surely as unruly as all her inclinations where Lord Harcourt was concerned. Fortunately it was the day of the Presentation, and once she had rung for Jane, she resolutely put it out of her mind.

They left the house nearly two hours before the appointed time. The ride in Lord Cunnington's carriage to the Queen's House, down Regent Street and along the Mall, gradually grew slower and slower as more carriages joined the procession, until it stopped altogether. Elena, glancing out from behind the curtains of the carriage, was surprised to see crowds of people, some extremely well dressed, lining either side of the Mall all the way to the gate, watching them.

Lady Cunnington, who would present Elena, was regal in violet moiré trimmed with ivory Brussels lace. She sat across from Elena in the closed carriage and smiled at her proudly but sadly.

"Your dear mother should be here to see you, Elena. What a pity your father should catch such a chill that she decided she could not leave him. You are looking quite, quite lovely."

The compliment went over Elena's head completely, but the reference to her father's condition reminded her of her own concern two days ago when the letter from Lady Theresa had informed them of his illness. If it were as serious as her mother reported, she should not even be here, Presentation or no, but at her father's side. And though she knew Aunt Winifred would not have countenanced her desertion unless Sir John were on his deathbed, she was quite certain, right now, that she would prefer to be with him at Tyndale Green than participating in this useless royal ritual.

"Charlotte heard that some of the girls actually lose their breakfasts, they get so nervous," Elena said, voicing a fear she had not dared put in words before. "I should die if . . ."

"Nonsense, my dear, you will carry it off in fine fashion. Besides, you've scarcely eaten a thing all morning."

Which, Elena thought, was probably why her stomach felt so queasy now. She had been given a little watered brandy and a wafer at midmorning to fortify herself, but that had only added to her discomfort. Her hands perspired inside her gloves but her feet were cold. She hardly dared move for fear the plumes on her head would be knocked askew against the carriage ceiling. The weather was warm but overcast, somehow oppressive. Everyone had prayed it would not rain. Elena now prayed for the whole affair to be over.

"Tell me, Aunt Winifred, how it went when you presented your two daughters to the Queen," she suggested, to keep her mind off the coming ordeal.

Lady Cunnington had already told the stories, but she was delighted to tell them again: how Angelina had torn her delicate crepe train by sitting on it in the carriage, but Lady Cunnington had managed to pin it so satisfactorily with her own hat pin that no one ever knew; how Letitia had fainted dead away once the Presentation was over and they were back in the hall, and it had taken two footmen with smelling powders to revive her. "So you see, my dear, nothing is fatal. For Letitia is now happily married, despite her mishap. You will survive quite nicely, I'm sure."

Elena nodded, not at all reassured. And what

would her grand *faux pas* be? Nothing so easy as fainting. Surely she would be painfully conscious through every minute of it.

The ornate iron gate to the Queen's House, at the end of the Mall, had opened for them and the footman riding on the rear of the coach had presented their cards. The carriage was allowed to proceed up the drive to the red brick mansion with the white pillared portico. Then she was descending, helped by another footman, mindful of her train, her plumes, her fan, almost (not quite) twisting her ankle, remembering to carry herself proudly and gracefully as she climbed the steps to the imposing front door, her train over her arm.

The large reception hall was already filled with young girls in trains and plumes, their older, more composed sponsors, and those young women who had recently acquired the status of wives. The gilt-embossed ceiling and cornices, the huge crystal chandelier, the mirrors and tapestries on either wall, were lost on Elena as she looked about for Charlotte but failed to find her. "It will be nearly an hour before we are announced," Lady Cunnington promised her grimly. "Let me know if you feel faint. I brought my vinaigrette."

Excited whispers and subdued murmurs wafted around her, but Elena felt little inclined to take part in conversation. Her eyes kept drifting to the magnificent double doors, now closed, at the end of the hall, where two motionless footmen stood guard. Meanwhile, a bewigged, brocaded chamberlain circulated through the crowd, taking cards and lining up everyone in order of precedence. Once this was established, they were allowed to perch stiffly on the benches that lined the hall.

As they waited, Elena saw Charlotte enter with

THE UNWELCOME SUITOR

Lady Saxton. Their late arrival provoked an eddy of murmuring through the crowd and a frown from the chamberlain, who hurried forward to examine their credentials and place them. Charlotte, the despair of her mama and the deportment masters, looked as stiff and awkward in Court dress as she had known she would, and her face was a mask of grim martyrdom. Elena caught her eye and smiled encouragement across the room. Charlotte answered with a grimace and a slight shrug of her tense, bare shoulders.

Finally the footmen opened the doors and stood aside. Elena stood with the others and was carried along by a sudden, eager rush into the next room—an anteroom—after which they were halted before another set of doors and made to wait their turn, this time in tense silence.

At last those doors, too, opened, and one by one the names were called. After endless moments, Elena heard the chamberlain announce, "Lady Winifred Cunnington, ma'am."

Elena walked through the door after her aunt, releasing her train, to be taken by a footman and laid out behind her once she had gained the drawing room.

"Your Majesty, may I present my niece, Miss Elena Tyndale, daughter of Sir John Tyndale of Huntingdon."

"My dear."

Queen Charlotte was seated unobtrusively in the middle of the large, magnificently appointed room, her ladies and others of the royal family standing about her. Her dark gown was surprisingly simple and her only jewelry, other than her coronet, was an enormous diamond and ruby pendant sparkling on her chest. Elena fixed her eyes on the jewel as she rose from her low curtsy and prepared to take the Queen's hand. To her amazement the Queen unmistakably turned a cheek toward her instead. Without giving herself time to think, Elena brushed her warm lips against the wrinkled cheek, then backed away.

"Enchantink," the Queen noted in her German-accented English, nodding approval.

"Thank you, your Majesty," Elena murmured, though her throat had turned quite dry and soundless.

She managed to back away from the Queen without becoming entangled in her clothing or tripping on the carpet, and dared to look about her. More jewels and medals gleaming against silk and brocade. More coronets. Princess Mary to the right, smiling. A curtsy. The Prince Regent—was that the Prince himself or one of his brothers, enormous and magnificent in scarlet and gold braid? Another curtsy. More blurred faces and jewels, more curtsies. She could turn now, she could leave the room.

Aunt Winifred was at her elbow, guiding her. "My dear, you did splendidly!" Suddenly her legs were weak. It was over.

Except, of course, that it was really just beginning. The next evening they were invited to Lady Wallingham's ball, where, Aunt Winifred warned her, Elena would be looked over by at least three of the six perpetual arbiters of Almack's, to see if she conducted herself well enough to be admitted to that exclusive establishment.

"What is so wonderful about Almack's?" Elena asked Lady Cunnington as Jane helped her into a dress of the finest pink muslin over peau de soie, with rows of exquisite lace set in the skirt.

THE UNWELCOME SUITOR

Lady Cunnington reviewed the results with a critical eye. "It is simply the one place anyone who is anyone must be seen, for it is very difficult to gain admittance," she explained. "One's dancing, as well as one's credentials, must be in perfect order. Jane, you missed the bottom hook in back. And do retie the sash. It needn't hold your mistress together, you know. Looser and more flowing will do."

Watching her image in the mirror as Jane fastened a pink feather in the nest of black curls, Elena decided she didn't care a fig whether she was admitted to Almack's or not. However, she was excited by the prospect of her first Society ball, where she would be allowed to at last put into practice all those dancing lessons she had loved in Vienna.

"You will probably dance quadrilles and reels," Lady Cunnington told her on the way as the carriage turned down Bond Street toward Piccadilly. "Last year Lady Wallingham had not yet accepted the waltz, though it has been done at Almack's. I must admit I am as broad-minded as the next person, but it does seem a trifle *risqué*, allowing a man to hold you about the waist. It would put me quite out of mind of the steps."

Lord Cunnington, seated beside his wife and across from Elena, merely said "Humph," as though no one would be likely to ask Lady Cunnington to waltz, anyway.

"Oh, but, Aunt Winifred, the steps become automatic, they are so easy," Elena explained guilelessly.

"Then you have learnt it?"

"Indeed I have. The waltz was much admired in Vienna."

Her aunt raised her eyebrows at the questionable morals of Society on the Continent. Lord Cunnington surprised both women by saying, "If a waltz is played, I shall be most happy to dance it with Elena myself, if that will save her from some man's unwanted—uh—attentions."

"Indeed, Geoffrey," Aunt Winifred said dryly.

Both amused and touched (for her uncle was a singularly uncommunicative man), Elena smiled and thanked him, although she had no particular qualms herself about allowing a man to hold her about the waist. Unless that man should turn out to be Lord Harcourt.

Most of the day she had considered the prospect of meeting him at the ball and wondered what she would do if he asked her to dance while Aunt Winifred, who so approved of him, was standing next to her. Could she feign sudden debilitating pains in her legs or, perhaps, another headache? Maybe it would not need to be feigned; the mere sight of him would surely bring one on.

The Cunningtons and Elena arrived at the Wallingham establishment on Piccadilly around nine-thirty, fashionably late like everyone else. In the entry hall, where liveried footmen took their wraps, Elena recognized no one in the crowd of arrivals. But as she climbed the stairs to the second-floor ballroom, her fingers grew clammy under her elbow-length lace gloves and she began to feel a hovering sense of unease, like a bird in flight expecting the attack of a hawk she could not see. The hawk, of course, was Lord Harcourt, who did not seem to be present, at least not yet.

A series of men, from young to middle-aged, stout to lean, tall to short, were eager to sign their names to her tasseled program. Each one was first carefully introduced by Lady Cunnington and accepted for a dance with her approval. It was all very studied, very

THE UNWELCOME SUITOR 71

formal, and at the end of each number Elena hardly noticed the change in partners. Eligible young ladies were expected to dance with each gentleman only once, and the little talk they were able to exchange before and after each dance tended to be the same.

But when Mr. Stuart Jaeger bowed before her, she smiled with more than usual warmth because this was the man who had caught Charlotte's fancy. He was tall and big-boned and obviously country-bred, somewhat like Charlotte herself, with a heavy thatch of blond hair and blue-green eyes as clear and straightforward as a summer sky. Unfortunately, Elena's special smile and her cordial "I have been hoping to dance with you, Mr. Jaeger," was his undoing. He gazed at her throughout the quadrille with such unabashed adoration Elena worried that Charlotte, from some part of the room, would recognize it. No, she wanted to say to him, I didn't mean that, I was only offering friendship.

Trying to remedy the situation, she said as he returned her to her aunt, "Have you danced with my friend Miss Saxton?"

He looked blank for a moment. "Miss Saxton? Oh, no, I don't believe I have."

"She is a dear," Elena said warmly. "You must see if she has any dances left."

His eyes questioned hers. "Very well," he said finally. "But first you must promise to allow me to take you in to supper."

"Oh, but, Mr. Jaeger . . ."

"Otherwise I shall not consider it worthwhile to dance with *anyone* else and shall leave immediately."

She was surprised at the authority in his voice. "Very well," she agreed reluctantly. "You may take me in to supper."

"Thank you." He bowed her gravely to her seat, then turned away. She watched him thoughtfully, disturbed by what she had unwittingly aroused and by the fact that he did not move toward Charlotte, whom she had just spied across the room.

"Miss Tyndale." Lord Harcourt's voice, startlingly close, was like a stab to her chest. Heat shot into her face. She glanced toward Lady Cunnington in some desperation, but her aunt was turned away and talking to a small, slender woman with fussy gray curls framing her face. Her next partner had not yet appeared, and she wondered why until she remembered there was to be a short intermission before the next dance.

So she had to look at him after all. He was dressed all in black and white, in the breeches and hose and buckled shoes that were only worn formally anymore. The severity of the colors made him seem taller, leaner, the latent danger of him somehow deadlier.

"Lord Harcourt," she murmured, afraid he could read the panic in her eyes.

She was sure he had when his expression turned to dismay. "I merely wished to pay my respects, Miss Tyndale."

"I . . . had not thought you were here," she responded lamely.

"We only just arrived. This is my mother . . ." And she realized that Lady Cunnington and the woman beside her had ceased talking and were looking their way.

"Mother," Lawrence said, beckoning to the petite woman, "may I present Miss Elena Tyndale, Lady Cunnington's niece."

"Lady Harcourt," Elena acknowledged with a little curtsy.

THE UNWELCOME SUITOR

"Oh, no, my dear Miss Tyndale, I am only Mrs. MacLean," Lord Harcourt's mother returned. "My dear late husband, being the younger son, was, unfortunately, never titled." She glanced toward Lawrence as though he ought to have conveyed this fact to Elena immediately. "Lawrence was kind enough to bring me along tonight. He was to have escorted his cousin, Lady Cordelia Radcliffe, but she was taken ill at the last moment."

Sensing a purposeful hostility in this information she did not understand, Elena was speechless.

Lady Cunnington put in, "Mrs. MacLean and I were at school together years ago, in Kensington, as I told you, Elena. I hadn't seen her in ages."

"Our land is too far north. It is difficult to travel to London from Northumbria, even in the best of weather," Mrs. MacLean explained. "Now, with Lawrence at Penton Hill, I suppose we shall be able to be in London oftener. I am sure Lawrence will have a great many new social obligations and need me to act as his hostess. At least until he marries." Her eyes slid over Elena and looked out to the rest of the crowded room, as though looking for a suitable bride to rescue her from the forthcoming exhausting duties.

"Mother and Lady Cunnington will wish to discuss old times," Lawrence said to Elena. He looked a trifle severe, and she thought his mother's attitude embarrassed him. "As for ourselves, Miss Tyndale, I would consider it an honor to be your partner for the next dance."

"Ah, well . . . I . . . believe it is spoken for, Lord Harcourt," Elena managed.

But Lady Cunnington, who held Elena's card for her, inspected it, "Not so, my dear. It is only Lord Cunnington, after all, and I am sure he will be relieved to leave it to another."

"Uncle Geoffrey? Are you sure, Aunt?" Elena asked in dismay.

Aunt Winifred ignored her distress. "Certainly, I'm sure. See for yourself. You recall we were surprised to see a waltz listed at all, and so he made good his little joke and agreed to partner you in it. Frankly, I doubt he has ever learnt the dance, and you will both be happier if you dance it with Lord Harcourt."

She smiled benignly at them, much as she had the night she had first introduced them, and Elena recognized with a racing heart that the trap was inescapable. It did not help to see the look of unmistakable animosity on Mrs. MacLean's face as Lawrence led her onto the floor.

7

She tried to gaze past him, as though he were any other dancing partner, and respond only to the music, to be less aware of his gloved hand at her waist, to forget that his eyes were constantly on her face. "I imagine I shall dare almost anything to make you mine." The words resounded in her brain, underscoring the lilt of the German waltz, taking her back to a chill walk around Cavendish Square, warmed by his appearance. You have no right to do this to me, she thought, and wished she dared say it out loud.

"You were very animated before, dancing the quadrille, Miss Tyndale. Cannot you favor me with the same charm you bestowed on my neighbor, Mr. Jaeger?"

The formality of his words mocked her. She felt a rush of anger and turned a cool gaze on him. "No, I cannot."

"Why not?"

"Lord Harcourt, I have asked you most specifically to leave me alone . . ."

"And I have done so, for a week and a half. Truly an age. But since we are present at the same ball, why should we not dance, just once?"

"You are not being fair."

His eyes grazed her face. "So the byword is to be 'fair'?" The words leapt at her, though his voice was soft enough. "Someday you will cease to mourn him. And when you do, I intend to be present."

She flushed, her steps faltered, and words utterly failed her. As she caught the beat again, he whirled her around in a breathless pirouette. "Don't be troubled, my sweet. Just dance."

His hand at her waist drew her imperceptibly closer. His expression seemed to lighten and smile, encouraging her to forget, to give in, to live *now*, in the present moment. She could no longer look away from his strange, beautiful eyes. His arms and his gaze guided her effortlessly into the intoxication of motion and sound until she floated on the music like driftwood on ocean waves. Words became intrusive, graceless. They only danced.

At the midnight buffet, where the crowd of over one hundred guests nibbled at meats and pastries, fruits and ices, and appeased their thirst with claret, hock, or spiced negus for the young unmarried ladies, Elena saw Charlotte Saxton for the first time. They were not close enough to speak, but Charlotte's eyes, observing Mr. Jaeger in close attendance on her, filled with reproach and she did not respond to Elena's unobtrusive wave. Elena silently promised her an explanation the following day, but she felt singularly guilty. Her attempt to put Mr. Jaeger off had been halfhearted. She had really welcomed his presence as a possible foil should Lord Harcourt have asked her for the same privilege. Simply because Lord Harcourt might be somewhere in the crowd, observing her, she had felt obliged to talk and laugh all the more animatedly with Mr. Jaeger.

She was relieved when, at last, the dancing resumed. Mr. Jaeger was forced to give Elena up to Mr. Mountjoy, who had escorted Charlotte Saxton to supper. I'm sorry, Elena tried to convey to Charlotte with her glance as the two faced each other directly for the first time that evening. Charlotte's greeting was grudging, barely civil, and Elena felt a pang of regret and hurt as she allowed Mr. Mountjoy to lead her into a reel. She heeded very little of what her partner said as they waited for the music to begin, and even less of her own responses, which were automatic rejoinders to Mr. Mountjoy's everlasting quips.

As the skips and bows and turns of the Scottish reel demanded her attention, Elena no longer took joy in the dancing. The colorful kaleidoscope of gowns and uniforms and jewels, the bright glow of the crystal chandeliers overhead, the increasingly stale, warm air of the long, gilded ballroom, began to weigh on her head. Only one dance, one moment had been worth the evening, and its magic had been far too intoxicating. "Someday you will cease to mourn, cease to mourn, cease to mourn..." I shan't, I shan't, she thought defiantly. I shall love Rodney forever. The music played on, interminable, and her feet were lead-weighted. She hoped she could persuade her aunt to leave as soon as it finished.

Mr. Mountjoy, too, seemed to find the atmosphere of the ballroom increasingly oppressive. His fingers dug a small trench between his high collar and his fat perspiring neck as the music mercifully ended. "So warm in here," he said to Elena. "Wouldn't you enjoy a turn in the garden?"

"My aunt . . ." Elena looked swiftly around the room for either Lord or Lady Cunnington, but they, very likely, were still in the anteroom or grouped about the buffet. Meanwhile, the prospect of a fragrant garden and cooling breezes beckoned her jangled nerves. "Yes, thank you, but only for a few minutes," she agreed. He guided her through the crowd to the staircase.

Once a footman had opened the veranda doors to the fresh air, Elena realized, with a disconcerting tremor, that the light from the house did not extend far into the dark garden. She considered turning back, but Mr. Mountjoy's hand at her elbow pressed insistently on. She continued down the white stone steps, reassuring herself that this was, after all, Mr. Mountjoy, whose main attractiveness was his inventive puns. He was tiresome at times but hardly dangerous. Right now his witticism about Society's passion for dancing in stuffy rooms on warm nights ("I myself prefer dry discourse to damp dancing") had her laughing appreciatively.

She was totally unprepared when he halted her behind the dark reaches of a forsythia bush with one hand on each of her arms. Facing him, she smelled, more strongly than before, the wine on his breath.

His voice came out hurried and blurred. "My dear Miss Tyndale, I have danced the reel for your sake. I would ask you only one boon in return."

She raised her eyebrows. "What is that, pray?"

"I am starving for a taste of those ravishing lips." And before she could react in surprise or revulsion, he had invaded her mouth with his own. She might have endured it for a moment, but once having seized his prize, Mr. Mountjoy had no intention of giving it up until he had taken his full. When his arms tried to draw her closer to his rotund body, she struggled and pulled away far enough to land a resounding slap on his cheek.

"Mr. Mountjoy! I thought you a gentleman!"

"My lady," he gasped, releasing her to nurse his

stinging face. "You led me to believe you might welcome a little sport." Even as he spoke, he grabbed her arm again. "Perhaps you are only bantering me . . ."

"No!" With a convulsive movement she threw off his grip and ran toward the veranda. Just outside its doors she nearly collided with a tall figure in black and white. Lord Harcourt.

Profound relief flooded her—an unaccountable emotion, given her recent decision about him.

"Oh, Lord Harcourt!" she cried out. "I . . . Have you seen Lady Cunnington?"

"I am quite certain she is not in the garden." The wryness of his voice purged her fear like a tonic. Mr. Mountjoy, who had halted his pursuit at Lawrence's sudden appearance, now approached, but he was no longer a menace.

"Good evening, sir," Lawrence said to him evenly.

Lionel Mountjoy sullenly continued past them into the house and did not reply.

Elena's eyes followed his disappearance into the mansion as she considered what explanation might mitigate her compromising behavior. "I . . . He suggested a stroll. I had no idea he would be . . . so . . ."

"I saw what happened," Lawrence said coolly. "If you had not gotten away from him, I should have interfered."

"You *saw*?"

"I saw you leave the ballroom with him. Forgive me—I followed. He has a dubious reputation and I feared . . ."

"And I thought him simply witty," she said ruefully. Then, realizing the import of his words, she added, "I suppose I should thank you."

"You sent him to grass most effectively." In the half-light she could only guess at his smile. "But if you'll forgive my saying so, your judgment concerning men could be improved."

"I don't take your meaning."

"Captain Farnsworth. And now Mr. Mountjoy, who, everyone knows, is a rake."

"I was not so informed. And what *about* Captain Farnsworth?" Her eyes challenged him; his glittered darkly in the dim light.

"How well did you know him?"

"Better than I know you. I suppose you will say my judgment of you is also poor."

"That depends... on whether you let your heart or your misconceptions do the judging."

They had walked a little away from the house as they spoke, as though it were natural to do so. His presence acted as a balm on her assaulted senses. She wanted to retort with some withering riposte, but his last gentle reproach forbade it. When she finally spoke, it was to herself as much as to him.

"It was wrong of me to come to London, no matter what my parents wanted. I have not recovered from my husband's death. And I cannot find amusement in all these entertainments."

"I believe you are more restored than you think you are."

She looked at him, startled. "How can you presume to know so much about me?"

He didn't answer right away. Instead, in a quick but gentle movement that left her no resistance, he folded her in his arms and laid his cheek against her hair. "Oh, my Elena, I know worlds about you. How, I'm not sure. If I could only make you see..."

If his presence had been balm, his embrace completed the healing. It held no selfish passion, no imposition of his greater strength, only an offering of himself as her shelter. For the first time that evening she was at peace. She longed not only to remain there but also to burrow even deeper into his embrace.

The sensation lasted only a moment. Voices and peals of laughter announced that more couples had deserted the ballroom and invaded the veranda. Elena withdrew and Lawrence made no attempt to hold her.

"I really must find Lord and Lady Cunnington, Viscount," she murmured.

"My name is Lawrence."

"I don't know you well enough . . ."

"You will. Meanwhile, you might as well get used to speaking my name."

His self-assurance, coupled with a tinge of humor, sent her heart fluttering into her throat. Half a dozen guests, anonymous in the shadow, poured out of the veranda doors, accompanied by a chorus of voices. Hoping the darkness hid her own face, Elena fled past them and into the house.

8

Elena awakened past noon the next day with the uneasy sense that she had disgraced herself the previous evening. It was mortifying enough that she had so misjudged Mr. Mountjoy's intentions that she had allowed herself to be alone with him in a dark garden; it was even more embarrassing to recall how she had allowed Lord Harcourt to embrace her and realize she had welcomed the embrace—and that from a man she had once considered anathema. It was, finally, painful to remember Charlotte's attitude: as though, by dancing with Mr. Jaeger and allowing him to escort her to dinner, Elena had somehow betrayed her friend.

That, at least, was something she could seek to rectify today. Reaching beyond the pink hangings of the bed, she rang for Jane, who brought her hot chocolate and the message that Lady Cunnington wished to see her.

"I suppose so," Elena said with a sigh, expecting to be read a lecture that would refer to her aunt's alarm when she had realized the night before that Elena had left the ballroom without her knowledge. She had, of course, made passing comment on it on the way home last night. Elena suspected she had thought of numerous ways to elaborate on the subject since then.

Instead, once she was seated against the pillows of her bed and sipping the hot chocolate, her aunt swept into the room with a bundle of invitations which she dropped in Elena's lap.

"You were a triumph last night, my dear! Invitations—not only to Almack's, but to the Princess de Lieven's soiree next week and even to Carleton House late in June. And a dozen others, some of which we'll need to turn down, because they simply aren't suitable or because of conflicting schedules."

Elena tried to smile. It would surely be rude of her to object further to her aunt's eager plans. Yet she couldn't help but compare this "triumph" with her overwhelming sense of inadequacy and reflect that the invitations had nothing to do with her personal inclinations.

"I'm glad I was a credit to you, Aunt Winifred."

Her aunt, seating herself in the brocaded boudoir chair nearby, regarded her with concern. "Where is your enthusiasm, my girl? Something is wrong. What is it?"

Elena only shook her head and began to sort through the elegantly scripted invitations, folded and sealed with the imprints of well-known coats of arms. All those invitations that proposed to fill the rest of her summer.

"Was there anything from my mother about Papa's condition?" she asked.

"Oh, yes, there was, yesterday. Didn't I show it to you? I intended to. He is much better. It was only a cold, after all. Theresa could easily have attended your Presentation. She worries too much about him." Lady Cunnington's own offhand relationship to Lord Cunnington, which had never developed beyond the first passing affection, made her a trifle impatient with her sister's devotion to Sir John.

"I thought perhaps I should go home for a few days to see him."

"Nonsense, my dear, you cannot leave now. Of course I applaud your filial devotion, but this summer your duty is primarily to yourself. That is understood by everyone, even Sir John. Besides, it looked to me as if your attitude to Lord Harcourt had undergone a change last night." She smiled at Elena wisely. "I have every intention of encouraging such an inclination, my dear. I shall even take you to call on his mother, although I'll admit the two of us never quite got on."

Elena took refuge in stirring her cocoa. "Please, Aunt Winifred, don't put yourself out on my account. It was clear to me that Mrs. MacLean didn't like me, and my attitude to her son really has not altered one whit."

"Tush, Elena." Lady Cunnington's voice was mildly reproving. "I'm not blind. I can see when two people are head over ears in love. And you would not be marrying his mother, after all. We shall call tomorrow afternoon."

In love with Lord Harcourt? She certainly was not! Elena was so incensed with the idea that she nearly forgot her concern for her father or her decision to write Charlotte a note and ask whether she might explain herself in person. She remembered the latter after dressing and finishing a breakfast of boiled egg, tea, and toast on the veranda. When she wandered into Aunt Winifred's study to ask for notepaper, Lady Cunnington had to know who might be the recipient of the letter. Hearing Elena's explanation, her aunt tried to brush aside Charlotte's attitude.

"You must learn, my dear, not to take these things

THE UNWELCOME SUITOR

so to heart. You obviously did nothing wrong, aside from possibly being too free with your smiles. I daresay your looks will always drive men mad with passion and turn women green with jealousy, no matter how you behave."

Elena blushed hard. No one had ever put it to her so baldly before. "That's terrible!"

"Would you rather look a gorgon and end your days an old maid?"

"Perhaps," Elena said reflectively, "if it all is going to be such a problem. But then, I suppose if I had my rathers, I would prefer to be somewhere in between."

"What nonsense! You're one of the luckiest girls alive, to have that raven hair and that fresh complexion and those marvelous eyes. Beauty means power and influence if you learn to use it right. And not just in the bedroom, either."

Further embarrassed, Elena only said, "I would still like Ross to deliver this note to Miss Saxton. I shan't rest easy until he does."

"Very well, my dear. After you write it, put it here with my own correspondence and I'll see that it is sent."

Much too early Claxton had awakened his master in his rooms on Clarges Street. When Lawrence, responding at last to the bustle about the room—blinds opening, the coffee cup rattling in its tray, the squeak of the door, footsteps going out and in, the crackle of his copy of *The Morning Post* being unfolded—the sun was pouring in the window and the clock on the mantel said only ten-thirty.

Lawrence rarely slept late, but last night (or rather, this morning) he had not retired until three, and sleep had eluded him until long after the birds had begun their early-morning serenade. "What the devil . . ." he began with a yawn and a grimace.

"Good morning, my Lord. I hope you slept well."

"I didn't, but no matter. Did I tell you to call me this early? Do I have some appointment?"

"No, my Lord, except you did say you intended to look in on the auction at Tattersall's. But I took the liberty . . . Frasier stopped by and asked me to deliver this note from Mrs. MacLean at the earliest opportunity." Claxton, a rotund, proper little man whom Lawrence had inherited from his uncle along with Penton Hill, advanced and proffered the letter.

"Put it on the table," Lawerence said, yawning. "I'll read it as I breakfast. And you could pour me some coffee now. You've gotten me half-awake; you may as well finish the job."

"Very good, my Lord," Claxton returned imperturbably, ignoring the implied reproach.

Thoughtfully Lawrence drank the strong coffee—a habit he had acquired in Spain when early rising and instant alertness were both necessary and disagreeable. He had acquired a number of habits in Spain, and one of the less admirable ones, according to Mrs. MacLean, was his failure to consult her on every major decision he made. This was not the first letter she had written him concerning some breach of filial duty that he was not even aware he had committed. What would she have to say this time?

Except for this one thing—her constant interference in his affairs—Lawrence was quite content to be out of the Army, which had occupied six years of his life, and to be deep now in plans to renovate Penton Hill, a property more run-down than he had expected. He had meant it when he told Elena that he never enjoyed killing any living thing, Frenchmen included. Yet the Army had conditioned him in a number of useful ways. At times almost living in the saddle, he had become physically strong and adaptable, sleeping and eating well under almost any conditions. He had learned to do disagreeable tasks efficiently without flinching. He had learned to both give and take orders. Realizing he must take full responsibility for those he gave, he had studied military tactics and invented a few of his own to spare the lives of his men whenever possible. That peculiar obsession had been a particular sore point between him and Captain Farnsworth, who was prone to opt for glory and dash instead of sound tactics. Farnsworth's reputation for unnecessarily risking lives had been notorious, even among a service where most recruits were considered little more than cannon fodder by their aristocratic officers. One such incident had led to a near-duel between the two men, stopped only by the interference of their commanding officer.

But Farnsworth had been careless in more than war, Lawrence recalled as he donned the buff-colored pantaloons of his morning suit. He was always swept away by the impulse of the moment. It was not surprising, really, that he had eloped with Elena Tyndale, even when he was legally married to the Portuguese girl he had gotten pregnant. He had probably forgotten his wife's existence, at least momentarily. Or else he had thought, in his woolly-headed way, that an English gentleman should not have to consider a shotgun marriage binding, once he had left foreign shores and returned home. Farnsworth had always expected life to treat him well. Whenever he was called to account for a hasty or ill-conceived action, he railed at life's unfairness and expected either his privileged rank or some close friend to bail him out.

Thank God I did kill him, Lawrence thought in a moment of savage anger—and was amazed at the violent reversal of his attitude. Always before, the memory of that night had resulted in a mental wince at what he had done, however unwittingly, especially when he considered the grief it had caused Elena. But upon confronting the alternative, he realized that Farnsworth, had he lived, would by now have made Elena's life miserable. With him dead, she at least had the opportunity to forget him and make a better second choice.

It occurred to Lawrence that had he met Elena and known the story of her elopement in his self-righteous youth—at nineteen, as a fledgling ensign in Portsmouth, for instance, or even in Spain and Portugal, where he looked with suspicion on any beautiful woman because of one woman's perfidy—he would have avoided her as though she were a minion of the devil.

But last year, when the Army had been in Paris after Waterloo, he had met a noble lady who, widowed herself, had not been afraid to teach him about women and about love. The lovely Madame L'Heureux, ten years his senior, had accepted his tentative adoration and, finally, his lovemaking, even as she had warned him it would not last. There would be another woman someday, she had consoled him with a gentle smile during their final good-bye. You'll recognize her, never fear. And she had been right, for now there was Elena.

Elena. Somehow he had recognized in her the same gift for sincerity and compassion that had drawn him to the French noblewoman. He stared at his face in the mirror of his dressing table as he shaved, nearly cutting himself as he recalled her sweetness in his arms. That wonderful sensation, brief as it had been, had kept him awake the rest of the night. That and the compelling need to know how she had reacted, once she had left him. Was she angry again, resentful that he had taken advantage of the situation, or had she really been as receptive as she had seemed? And the way they had danced the waltz, as one person, as light and air mingling and floating above waves . . .

His hand trembled and a thin red line gleamed on his jaw. Wounded for love, he thought with a wry grimace. He swore and reached for the towel, wiped away the blood along with the soap, and held out his arms so Claxton could help him into his cambric shirt.

Mrs. MacLean had written the letter immediately after returning from the ball. When only into the first sentence, Lawrence realized that he should have known better than to read it while he ate his breakfast.

My dear Lawrence, [he read]

It all came clear to me tonight—why you have chosen to abandon poor, dear Cordelia. I guessed it when you introduced me to Miss Tyndale (a mother's heart can see more than you'll ever imagine!), but especially, I saw it as you danced with her. I can only pray that the whole of Society does not realize by now that you have lost your senses entirely.

Before you label me an alarmist, I want you to think quite carefully about what you really feel for this Miss Tyndale and decide whether she is worth possible scandal. Yes, I know, she is presentable and of good family, although, as I recall, the Tyndale property is small and her father, who is only a baronet, is not particularly well off. Still, I would not object if that were all. But as the ball neared its conclusion last night, I recalled something Lady Lampert had told me in regard to Miss Tyndale. (I have, as you know, an excellent memory for names.) They met last September at Cheltenham, where Miss T. had quite obviously taken a *tendre* for a dashing cavalry captain, as flighty girls are apt to do. When the captain disappeared from the scene, rumor had it he had eloped. Surely you heard it, too, for you were there at the time, were you not? Anyway, according to my memory of it, everyone was given to believe that Miss T. had taken ill and returned home the very day after the elopement. A common fib! It is quite obvious she is the girl the captain eloped with. If not, why did she then seclude herself in the country for the better part of nine months? (*And*, my dear Lawrence, why *do* young, unmarried—and *foolish*—women seclude themselves from Society for such a length of time? Think about this.)

If you are only planning an *amour*, I'm sorry to have troubled you. If you are actually thinking of making this woman your wife, you must, my dear son, consider the consequences of admitting a woman of soiled reputation (if not now, it *will* be, you know) to the sanctum of the Harcourt title and holdings. You do owe a duty to your position in life. You have spoken more than once about going into politics, once Penton Hill is running smoothly. If you want to be a power in government, your reputation—and that of your spouse—must be irreproachable . . .

THE UNWELCOME SUITOR

"Rot!" Lawrence muttered aloud. He crushed the letter savagely in his hand and threw it across the room toward the unlit fireplace. A few minutes later, his breakfast unfinished, he left the house.

9

Mrs. MacLean was not at home. Since she rarely went out before noon, Lawrence suspected she had deliberately absented herself to avoid confronting him over the letter. The thought that she might begin repeating her suspicions of Elena to her friends (and it seemed quite clear her letter had threatened it) horrified him.

Not at home, said Frasier, answering the door. Lady Cordelia was home but still abed after a poor night, and probably sleeping. Lawrence left a note of sympathy for her, remounted Starlight, and went on his way.

At Hyde Park Corner he waited for Tattersall's noon auction to begin. He had thought to find a hunter to replace the one he had shot at Tyndale Green, but he could not concentrate on the choice examples of horseflesh that were paraded before his eyes. His very reason for being there reminded him of Elena—of coming face to face with her on that spring-green hillock as she stood in the sun, shading her eyes with her hand, her astonishing beauty dropping, goddesslike, into the dark river of his anger and frustration.

The horses all seemed either too young and skittish, past their prime, or simply overpriced. After an hour's milling about, enduring the crowd's jostling and the urgings of the sellers without seeing an animal of real promise, he gave it up as a bad job and went on to Lord's, where, again, his mind refused to take in the intricacies of the cricket game being played. Avoiding the professional bettors at the pavilion, he placed a private wager on the outcome with a friend he chanced to meet, but did not wait to see the game finished.

By then his intention of returning to his mother's for afternoon tea, to force her to explain her attack on Elena, no longer seemed a good idea. The more interest he showed in Elena, the more opposed to her Mrs. MacLean would be. He would have to think of a roundabout way to make her more amenable, for the issue was far too important to risk an irreconcilable clash with her.

As the day waned, Lawrence realized that all his mother's insidious criticisms ("as flighty girls are apt to do" . . . "a woman of soiled reputation") were having their effect on him, if only to make him think more deeply about what it was, exactly, that had made Miss Elena Tyndale the dearest object on earth to him. The impulsiveness that his mother called flighty seemed to him only a sign of her unquenchable honesty. An impulsive person was unable to dissemble, to flirt and cheat, as had a certain lady in Portsmouth. And perhaps all he and Elena needed, now, was more honesty between them, especially on his part. Only in that way could she know him well enough to see beyond the part he had played in Farnsworth's death.

He was having a drink with a fellow club member at Brooks's when he decided what to do next. Instead of staying for supper as usual, he excused himself and went to his rooms. He needed time and solitude to think out the letter he wanted to write.

Jane brought the letter to her mistress the following morning, with her hot chocolate. Reluctantly at first, then with an eagerness she could not suppress, Elena read:

My lovely Elena,

You will say I don't know you well enough to address you thus, and that is true; yet I cannot refrain from it. Why do I feel I have known you for centuries, and how can I convince you that my feelings are deep and sincere?

Those same feelings possessed me at Lady Wallingham's and gave me the audacity to hold you in my arms, if only for a minute. Yet you did not object, and before we parted, your words were gentle. I can only hope this means your attitude toward me is changing.

You have said that your aversion to me was based solely on my unhappy connection to the death of Captain Farnsworth. Though reluctant to remind you of it, it will, possibly, help to erase that aversion if I explain just what happened that night last September. If such recollection is still too painful for you, stop now, throw this letter away, and don't answer it. But if, as I halfway suspect, you have some small portion of feeling for me, you will read all of this and answer my question at the end of it.

Back, then, to that unfortunate night. I was traveling from Cheltenham, where I had spent a few days with friends (and where I first laid eyes on you), to Crafton Hall in Northumbria, where my mother lives the better part of the

THE UNWELCOME SUITOR 95

year. I had only recently sold out of the Army and had not been in England for several years. It was both surprising and disconcerting that I should have chosen the same inn as did you and Captain Farnsworth that night, to escape the rainstorm.

Let me make clear that Captain Farnsworth and I were not on good terms, thanks to some things that happened between us during the Peninsula campaign three years before. However, our meeting was amiable enough, and we were sharing a bottle of porter when I mistakenly alluded to those happenings. Details here are unimportant; what transpired after that is simply that our argument grew heated and he attacked me, jumping over the table and gripping my throat. In my struggle to free myself, I knocked him against the stones of the fireplace mantel, and from there, he nearly fell into the fire and cut his forehead and eye on the fender, going unconscious.

I pulled him away as soon as I realized his danger, called the innkeeper and his wife to tend him, and went for the surgeon with my own horse, since no other animal was available. But, as you know, we were too late to save him.

I have suffered mightily from it since then, not only because I dealt a death blow (however inadvertently) to him, but also because I made no attempt to meet you that night and extend my heartfelt apologies.

Now you have my account of that damnable event. Read it and judge whether or not I deserve a chance to make amends for the injury I did you that night. If your generous spirit can forgive me, if you can put aside the past, I would ask only one thing of you—another opportunity to see you and talk to you, and if you are willing, to show you what is in my heart. Will you, this time, say "yes" to an old invitation? Hyde Park is fresh and lovely at sunrise, without people or traffic. We could ride along Rotten Row tomorrow as fast or as slow as you wish, with whatever companion you think appropriate. Have you a horse? If not, I'll gladly provide one from my stables. If you agree, do me the kindness of responding today. And always, I beg you, consider me

Ever your most obedient & devoted servant,
Lawrence

Elena's cheeks were hot as she read the letter the first time. The second time, some minutes later, when her pulse was again under control, she read it more slowly and pondered especially the account of the quarrel. It was the unexplained portions—the why of it all—that cried for an explanation. What had Lord Harcourt said when he "alluded to those happenings"? What were the happenings? Of what had he accused Rodney, for an accusation of sorts it must have been? Did the letter really exonerate Lord Harcourt or did it simply seek to excuse and thereby pave the way for his pursuit of her?

Why must it be me? she asked herself again. But this time the question swam in her head until it became, Why him? And she already knew the answer. Something flashed between them each time they met, and had, ever since that first encounter in the country. Both had recognized it, but she had fought it all along because of Rodney.

Not just because Lawrence MacLean had been responsible for Rodney's death. But because she had sworn to love Rodney to the death—her death, not his. And that vow, made implicity when she had run away to Gretna Green with him (for only a deathless love could justify such imprudent actions) and spoken in hushed voice before an anonymous clergyman, had been reinforced a hundred times by his untimely, appalling death.

So she thought, again, It's impossible, I can't love someone else, it would be a betrayal of Rodney, of our love. I mustn't listen to what is in this man's heart.

She called Jane to bring her writing paper and pen, donned her dressing gown, and sat down at her writing table. She intended to compose a terse little note refusing his invitation. Instead, she read his letter again and was once more struck with curiosity. Finally, after staring vacantly at the wall for a quarter of an hour, she wrote:

Dear Lord Harcourt,

I shall accept your invitation to go riding tomorrow morning because it is something I have dearly longed to do since coming to London. It seems very difficult for females here to get exercise of the sort I was accustomed to in the country. I would appreciate the loan of a mount. Lady Cunnington doesn't ride, and the carriage horses would not be suitable.

You see by this I have overcome my "aversion" to you. I am willing that we be friends, but only that, for I intend to remain true to my beloved husband's memory.

Thank you for telling me of the events leading to his death. I should have allowed you to tell me all this at the beginning of our acquaintance.

> By avoiding the issue I did you an injustice, for which I beg you to forgive me.
>
> Your explanation was not totally satisfactory, however. If we are, indeed, to be friends, should I not be allowed to know what led to the fight? You say details are unimportant. On the contrary, I believe they must have been crucial, and if they involved me in any way, I have a right to know about them.

She pondered long and hard as to her complimentary close and finally added, "My thanks for your kind invitation" and her full name. She hoped the letter would set the proper tone for their meeting —friendly and yet composed. Her refusal to even refer to that brief embrace in the garden should show him that he should not read any significance into it.

She sealed the letter quickly with wax and gave it to Jane to pass on to one of the footmen to deliver. When she told Lady Cunnington, at breakfast, of the invitation and her acceptance of it, her aunt made no attempt to hide her pleasure. "You will, then, be amenable to visiting Mrs. MacLean later today, Elena?" she suggested.

"If you think we should, Aunt Winifred."

"I do, indeed. I fear I have long neglected her. I'll admit she struck me as too top-lofty and too easily provoked in our salad days, but perhaps time has mellowed her. We had quite a delightful chat the other evening. At any rate, it can only help matters if she and you become better acquainted."

"Simply because I'm going riding with Lord Harcourt does not mean I intend to marry him," Elena said.

Lady Cunnington only smiled.

THE UNWELCOME SUITOR

* * *

Charlotte Saxton's two blue parakeets, freed of their cage, flew about the small conservatory on the south side of the Saxton residence; then, at their mistress's whistle, alighted, one on her shoulder, one on her proffered left wrist.

Elena was delighted. "How can you train them so beautifully?"

"With patience—and plenty of tidbits," Charlotte said. The demonstration had helped restore an equilibrium between them. In a setting like this—away from the glittering ballroom world in which Elena had been such a success two nights before—Charlotte was clearly in her element.

"Even so . . . " Elena pursued in wonder. She had not been allowed any pets because, in Lady Theresa's view, they were never quite clean. Such obedience from mere birds seemed to her little short of magic.

"I've trained horses and dogs; birds are not really so different," Charlotte said casually. She smiled at Elena, welcoming her awe. It had been far different when the visit had begun. There had been several awkward moments as Elena had felt obliged to apologize for allowing Mr. Jaeger to take her in to supper at Lady Wallingham's ball. Charlotte had said, sharply, that there was no need to apologize, but Elena, sensing her resentment, had persisted.

"You mustn't hate me for it, that's all. I value our friendship."

Charlotte had shrugged. "I know it's not your fault. Even though, later, he spoke of you all the time he was with me."

"How very thoughtless of him!"

"Yes, wasn't it? Still, how can I blame him? He's no better at hiding his feelings than I am." Charlotte had smiled at her ruefully, the first sign that she was thawing. Elena's admiration at Charlotte's mastery over her birds had done the rest. Before they parted, Charlotte impulsively hugged her and, taking advantage of the good-byes between Lady Cunnington and Lady Saxton, whispered, "And you—are you interested in Lord Harcourt?"

"He . . . he is really Aunt Winifred's idea," Elena stammered.

Charlotte's smile grew wistful. "Are you sure that's all? You danced so beautifully together the other night."

Elena wondered how many others had viewed the dance that way.

Mrs. MacLean wondered the same thing. And if the sight had led her to suspect the identity of the young lady who had stolen Lawrence's heart, she knew she had guessed rightly when Lady Cunnington and her niece called.

"Lady Cunnington thinks to soften me on Miss Tyndale's behalf," she told Lady Cordelia once their visitors had left after an uncomfortable twenty-minute chat about trifles. "But I have a long memory and it simply won't wash. She always snubbed me when we were at school, just because her father was titled and mine wasn't. She ignored my at-home invitations when I first married the Colonel, which I only sent her because of our old school association, and now that her niece has eyes for my son, she believes it will help if she makes up to me. Well, it won't."

Though small of stature, Mrs. MacLean was formidable in resentment. Her pronounced chin jutted out even farther, and her brown eyes were afire as she spoke.

Lady Cordelia sat very still during this, her gaze on the petit-point pillow cover she was working, her needle very busy. Pale fine hair curled around her slender face, which was more wan than usual because of her recent illness. At last she said meekly, "Forgive me, my dear cousin, but do you not think it the least little bit up to Lawrence, after all?"

"Certainly it is up to Lawrence, but he always regarded you most favorably—*most* favorably—until this black-haired siren crossed his path. I have never favored dark-haired women. They are all too often either triflers or tartars."

"Especially when they are beautiful, I suppose," Cordelia mused softly.

Mrs. MacLean eyed her sharply. She loved Cordelia dearly and had done so ever since the girl had come to live with them when she was twelve, but she did think that at times, like now, she wanted spirit. "You don't seem to care. I thought you loved Lawrence."

"Of course, Cousin Alice. I always have and I always shall love him," Lady Cordelia replied. "And I have always been grateful to you for taking me in when I was an orphan and treating me as your daughter, but that never meant your son would necessarily think of me as his future wife. I am accustomed to waiting and . . ."

"And being grateful for crumbs," Alice MacLean leapt in with indignation. "And you deserve so much more! Sometimes I think you positively forget that you are the daughter of an earl and a countess in your own right. Or that you will come into a great deal of money when you are turned twenty-one. And you are lovely, too, child. You have far too modest an opinion of yourself. At any rate, if I can't have you for a daughter-in-law, I shall have no one."

At this onslaught Cordelia shrank back in her chair and said nothing. Mrs. MacLean rose restlessly and went to the wall to ring for a maid to clear away the tea things. After a long silence Cordelia finally dared to say, "I do not see what we can do, in any case. But Miss Tyndale did not seem to me to be overly attached to Lawrence."

"It's a pose, of course. She's being very discreet and agreeable." Mrs. MacLean spoke thoughtfully as she looked out the window to the street below. Then she turned back to Cordelia abruptly. "There is a great deal we can do. She would be very unsuitable for Lawrence and I've told him so. There are these rumors I've heard . . ."

"But none is really substantial . . ."

"No, but they could be, they could be."

"I don't see . . ."

Mrs. MacLean turned back to Lady Cordelia with a little frown. "You forget my friend, Lady Lampert, the one who told me of Miss Tyndale's infatuation last autumn for that cavalry captain. There was most definitely talk of scandal at the time, especially when they both left Cheltenham at the same time. That it has died down only shows how quickly people forget. Add to that the length of time since, and Miss Tyndale's rather sudden appearance in London's drawing rooms, during the height of the Season—why, it is almost as though some obligation had prevented her coming earlier."

"Still . . ." Lady Cordelia ventured hesitantly.

But she was no match for her older cousin. "*I* find it quite simple to put the pieces together from all this, if you do not, child, and I find it appalling that this Miss Tyndale should have her sights fixed on Lawrence. Ordinarily I pay gossip no mind, but if my son's future happiness is at stake, I have a certain duty. You may safely leave everything to me."

She nodded her head and smiled confidently at the girl.

Lady Cordelia surrendered her eyes to the safety of her needlework.

10

London just past dawn was a new world for Elena. The streets belonged now to vendors of breads and fruit, to bucket-laden milkmaids, to mob-capped servants scrubbing their master's front stoops, polishing brass door knockers and wrought-iron lamp posts, shaking dust mops out the dark stairwells that climbed up to street level from basement kitchens. Near Baker Street workmen coated with dust were digging up paving stones and earth to lay pipes for the new miracle of lighting, gas. Farther on, a squad of palace guards in scarlet tunics and black bearskin hat marched by, returning to barracks after the night watch. The carriages that passed, with curtains drawn against daylight, carried the sleepy remnants of revelers from the gambling tables of Jermyn Street or the brothels and taverns of Covent Garden and Soho. Droplets of sun-shot dew, suspended in the cool fresh air, wrapped everything in an evanescent, golden haze.

None of it seemed quite real to Elena—neither the surprising bustle at an hour when she was usually asleep; nor the motion of the horse, a pretty bay named Taffy, under her; nor the presence beside her

THE UNWELCOME SUITOR

of the man in riding boots and green hunting jacket on his mottled gray. Elena herself wore the old blue gabardine habit she had brought with her from Tyndale Green, since Lady Cunnington had not thought to include riding wear in her new wardrobe. The pert white-feathered hat that sat on her black hair matched and brought out the blue of her eyes.

Elena had not slept well, anticipating the ride and the man, rehearsing carefully her attitude, her words, her excuses to herself for having agreed to this outing. Now attitude and excuses had fled. With the first glance from his eyes and the first greeting from his lips she realized that a casual, friendly outing with Lord Harcourt would be impossible. By then it was too late to back down.

His eyes, mostly amber this morning, reflecting the glittering pale light, were quite openly warm and tender whenever he looked at her. The hand he offered when she mounted shook momentarily at her touch and then was reluctant to release her to the sidesaddle. He seemed to be, for the first time in their acquaintance, quite tongue-tied, while she, scarcely daring to look at him, concentrated on getting used to the horse. Elena wondered what Ross, who followed at a discreet distance, mounted on one of Lord Cunnington's hacks, thought of their silent passage through the early-morning streets.

They entered Hyde Park at Brook Gate and took a graveled path between the trees to Rotten Row, that traditional bridle path of sedate horsemanship, moving side by side, yet making no effort to talk. She could feel his presence like a flame that seared her skin. Nothing she considered saying to him seemed logical or worthwhile or disinterested enough. Yet, as ecstatic birdsong echoed her beating heart and newly blossoming roses scented the air, she was sane enough to admit she wanted to be nowhere else on earth.

It took the sight of a small family of deer, grazing only a short distance from the path, to break the silence.

"Oh, look!" Elena pointed out in low tones of wonder, halting her horse. "And two little fawns."

Lawrence stopped almost simultaneously with her and looked, but his eyes returned soon to her rapt face. "An ideal family," he noted. "The buck is young —see how small his antlers are."

The deer, aware of their presence but not really startled, lifted their heads one by one, then moved on into the trees. "I have never understood how people can shoot them for sport," Elena said as she urged her horse on again.

"Sportsmen haven't your sense of awe—or of pity," he suggested.

She turned to him. "Do you shoot deer?"

"I never have. Grouse, sometimes. And fox hunts, though I prefer the chase to the kill."

"Somehow foxes are different," Elena conceded, "though I pity them, too, when they are caught."

Their eyes met—an indiscretion, for he smiled, wordless again, and the invitation in his glance was unmistakable. She dropped her gaze and tried to hide the awkwardness of the moment with further conversation.

"My aunt and I called on your mother yesterday."

"Oh?" Lawrence's tone was surprised and a little wary. "Was it an enjoyable visit?"

Elena laughed. "I don't know. It was ... strained, I daresay. She seemed most cool to me. Polite, but cool. I think she mislikes me, but I'm not sure why."

"Because she knows I've set my heart on winning you, and she has other ideas."

Elena's cheeks burned. "How does she know? Did you tell her?"

"No, I never uttered your name. It must have been the way we danced together."

"Oh, that wretched dance!"

"Why wretched? Didn't you enjoy it?"

"Everyone saw . . ." She hesitated.

"Yes? What did they see?" he asked quickly.

She glanced at him, then away again, shaking her head. "Tell me about Lady Cordelia," she said after a moment. "Is she a relative?"

There was a slight silence, as though he was disappointed at the turn the conversation had taken. "Yes. She's a second cousin on my mother's side. She has lived with us for seven years, ever since her parents died."

"And your mother wants you to marry her?" Elena guessed.

The silence this time was much longer. "Yes," Lawrence said at last. "I won't lie to you."

"Then why haven't you done so? Were you about to before you met me?"

"No, I was never about to marry Lady Cordelia."

"Why not?"

"I don't love her," he said evenly, the edge of his patience showing. "I think of her as a cousin and a friend. Only that."

"I thought she was pleasant," Elena mused. "But she didn't say much."

"Exactly. She never says much. She lets my mother do all her talking. My mother walks all over her, as she will with anyone who will let her. The only way Cordelia would have a life of her own is to marry someone far removed from Mother and live in . . . Ireland or perhaps Canada. We are not suited, Cordelia and I. Someday Mother will accept that."

"That's why she was so . . . aloof then," Elena said thoughtfully.

"Very likely." After a minute he added, "I'm sorry. But you needn't worry about pleasing my mother. I very rarely do . . . because it's impossible."

Elena stiffened. "Excuse me, Lord Harcourt. You talk as if I think it a matter of some importance. I assure you I don't, since Mrs. MacLean and I will doubtless have little occasion to . . ."

"*You* talk as though we were in a drawing room full of strangers and had just met," he reproved her. "And do call me Lawrence. I thought we were to be friends."

"It is the lady's privilege to decide when it is appropriate to be so informal."

"I always call you Elena in my thoughts."

"You are very bold."

"You already know that."

Elena hesitated, feeling her way. "You read my note . . ."

"Every word."

"I said we were to be friends rather than . . . more than that. I tried to make you understand I probably will never marry again."

"At least not to a man you love."

"What do you mean by that?"

"Society—and your family especially—won't allow you to go widowed the rest of your life, Elena. It's preposterous. And so, someday, you'll give in, and I predict it will be to some stodgy old widower. You will marry him because you'll have no cause to compare him to your dead husband. So you needn't

THE UNWELCOME SUITOR 109

break whatever absurd vows you made to love him forever."

She was shocked, not only by his prediction but by the perception of his last sentence. But the stormy words she wanted to utter would not come out.

"If you loved him so dearly, how much better to marry a man you *can* compare him with," Lawrence went on, a flippant tone entering his voice.

"Like you, you mean?"

He grinned. "Exactly. After all, you must admit he and I had the same taste in women."

"I think you are being rather horrid."

His face sobered. "I don't intend to be. I just want you to think seriously about what you are doing. Because I assure you everyone will do their utmost to see you married. Your beauty makes you a danger to every woman in London. And, after all, isn't that why your family sent you to London?"

"I simply agreed not to 'mope' any longer, as my mother put it."

"And to attend routs and meet eligible young men, who are bound to become enraptured with you on sight and try to make up to you, as Mountjoy did..."

"Oh, why must you sink me with *that*?"

"So you will face reality."

"I don't..." She was trembling and hot and her eyes brimmed with tears. She wiped them away with the back of her glove unthinkingly, averting her gaze.

The childish gesture caught at Lawrence's heart. Yet he refused to apologize for his harshness. Instead, after giving her a moment to regain control, he suggested a swift canter around the loop. She glanced at him with hurt eyes, then let out a big sigh and unexpectedly smiled. "All right. A race, then."

"Is that quite fair?"

"To you or to me?" Her riding crop slashed down on the horse's rump, and Taffy took off. She heard Lawrence's startled exclamation, felt his horse gaining on her, and urged her own mount to greater speed. The fresh wind zinging past her cheeks and the sensation of nearly flying, being at one with the horse, restored her. She gave Taffy his head and allowed him to break into a full gallop. They passed the starting place and headed into the loop again. Lawrence had not caught up with her and she was defiant and exultant. As she rounded the last curve a second time, Taffy slowed of his own accord. Noticing Ross, stock-still on the hack a short distance off the path, Elena pulled in rein and stopped near him.

"I'm sorry, Ross. You aren't used to riding, are you?"

"It's not that, ma'am," the footman said, going red, "so much as that I'm expected to act as a sort of . . ."

"Chaperone, yes, I know. But his Lordship could hardly accost me at *that* breakneck speed, could he?"

"And breakneck it was, too," Lawrence gasped, bringing in Starlight just in time to hear her last words.

She favored him with a glance of mock concern. "A thousand pardons, Lord Harcourt. I fear I did not give you adequate warning."

"I hope you will consider us quits then, Miss Tyndale." They moved their horses into a walk again, this time side by side.

Warmed by her brief sense of victory, Elena gave him a generous smile. "Now, Lord Harcourt, before you return me to Queen Anne Street, I have a question for you. A serious one."

"My name is Lawrence," he reminded her. "It is the only name I will answer to."

THE UNWELCOME SUITOR

She was taken aback, but continued on bravely. "Very well . . . Lawrence." A thrill zipped through her as she said it, momentarily stopping her. "I ask you then, as a friend, to tell me about your relationship with Captain Farnsworth. Tell me why you quarreled with him."

She had obviously taken him by surprise. And instead of falling in with her frank mood, his lips set in a hard uncompromising line, reminding her of his look the day they first met.

"There are some things it is not appropriate for one gentleman to say of another," he said finally.

"But you have asked me, more than once, how well I knew him. I will confess, not well at all—only enough to love him, enough to . . . At any rate, you spoke in your letter of happenings in Portugal . . ."

"He is dead now, Elena. Let it rest. It will do you no good to know."

She saw that nothing was going to change his mind, but that did not prevent her from crying out, "Then I collect it's something that would reflect on *you* rather than on him! Or you would tell me and exonerate yourself."

"And be branded as wholly self-serving in your eyes," he said.

"Why? Why would it be, if it's the truth?"

"I'm sorry. I cannot tell you. Not now, at any rate."

As she continued to stare angrily at him, he leaned forward suddenly, grabbed her horse's bridle, and brought them both to a standstill. Then, quickly, he dismounted and came around to lift her down from her horse. She allowed him to help her dismount, her eyes questioning his serious, determined face. "What do you . . ."

His hands still holding her arms, he said very quietly, "What happened between Farnsworth and myself is not important. Not anymore. All that matters is here—between you and me. You must look at what is happening between us—and it *is* happening—now, with clear eyes, without letting the past obscure it. It's real, Elena. *Now* is what's real for us. Not the past."

She tried to clutch her anger to her, but the solemn assurance of his words made the emotion seem unworthy. The gold flecks dancing in his eyes drew from the depths of her body a long shivering pulse that resonated from her temples to her toes. She could do nothing but stand there and absorb the sensation.

Then he drew her into his arms and kissed her deliberately, lingeringly, as though they were in the most private chamber of a secluded house and not on a public bridle path. She did not resist; she did not even protest when he finally released her. She suspected that she had actually kissed him back.

"I . . ." she began weakly, wanting to reiterate her claim to a lost love. But the words would not come out. Instead, she only felt herself drowning in the tenderness of his gaze. "You had better take me back," she managed.

"Yes. Anything more would spoil it." He helped her remount and they turned their horses around. Ross was waiting for them at the entrance to the path, his face studiedly turned to a bed of pansies. He had, of course, seen everything and would report it to Lady Cunnington. Elena had an idea her aunt would be delighted.

It was the afternoon Aunt Winifred had established as her at-home. A number of the young men Elena had met at the musicale and Lady Wallingham's ball, perhaps even some who had seen her at the theater, could be expected to pay short visits. Elena, the disturbing magic of the morning ride remaining with her long after its finish, had entirely forgotten this. When reminded at lunch by her aunt, she was unimpressed, seemed, in fact, moody and distracted.

"You enjoyed your ride, I trust?" Lady Cunnington asked. She already knew about the kiss, but if she hadn't, Elena's preoccupation would have hinted at something of the sort.

"Oh, Aunt Winifred, I should never have gone with him."

"Nonsense, child."

"It is not nonsense. And I'm not a child any longer, more's the pity."

"You would prefer to remain stunted?" her aunt asked dryly.

"It's this . . . beauty thing," Elena said at last, her voice near a whisper. "Do you think Lord Harcourt would pay attention to me if I weren't what everyone calls 'beautiful'? Would Rodney—oh, Aunt, I never before thought of it—but would Rodney have wanted to elope with me if I hadn't been beautiful? And all those gentlemen coming today . . . how many would there be if I were plain? What about a dear girl like Charlotte Saxton, who is a marvel with birds and animals? Yet the man she loves pays court to *me*. It's not fair. It's *awful*. And Lord Harcourt. If it weren't for me, he would probably settle down happily enough and marry his cousin, Lady Cordelia Radcliffe, as his mother wishes. I expect Lady Cordelia adores him."

"You mustn't think of all those things, my dear. I'll grant you beauty can create problems, but so can a great many other things. You must just be very careful that your prospective husband is worthy of your own devotion. If you are a loving wife and not a tease or a flirt, your beauty will be beside the point. An asset but not your *raison d'être*."

"*That* doesn't signify, for I shan't marry. I just feel that instead of this social whirl, I should return home and . . ."

"Shan't marry! Oh, pooh, Elena."

"My love for Rodney was enough."

Lady Cunnington shrugged impatient shoulders. Finally, after advising a footman they would have desert now, she said, "Was he so tip-top, then, that no man on earth can match him?"

"He was to me."

"Oh, come now, my dear, no man is that. You must try to be objective."

"Well, he was . . . restless," Elena admitted at last. "But that was part of his charm. He was always eager to be planning and doing things. Daring things."

"Such as eloping? That shows only that he was contemptuous of Society, and perhaps even of you, my dear. He was so caught up in his own desires he never considered *your* welfare, your reputation. Proposing that you elope as you did—to my mind that was very wrong. If he had lived . . ."

"Rodney was to return to his regiment in France in two weeks. It was all the time we had. We feared . . ."

"Was a short separation so impossible? You could have been engaged for a time. He was well-enough-connected; any objections from family surely might have been overcome eventually. There is no war now, no reason to expect he would be killed once he rejoined the Army. Such haste was foolish and unseemly."

"Yes, I know! It was foolish and unseemly and . . .

headstrong. And no doubt a great many other things. But how can I regret that I loved him?"

She lowered her gaze to take a spoonful of the newly arrived blancmange, then looked up to see how her aunt had responded. Lady Cunnington's eyes were still on her, as though she viewed a perplexing problem that needed solving. Seeing Elena's glance, she smiled in a resigned sort of way and murmured, "Young people!"

Elena smiled back and attempted to reassure her. "I vow I shan't dwell on the past anymore, Aunt. You have taught me *that* lesson. But regarding Charlotte, I am truly concerned. And I have a thought to help her. I know you will say I shouldn't interfere, but I hope you will allow me to pursue it . . ."

11

"And what may I do for you, Miss Tyndale?"

Mr. Jaeger's blue-green eyes looked as though he would be willing to do a great deal, maybe conquer a few worlds for no one's sake but hers.

Elena stammered a noncommittal answer and looked away, not quite certain how to handle the situation. She had asked Mr. Jaeger to remain after her other visitors to the at-home had left.

"I-it is so dismal and dark in the house. Shall—shall we take a turn in the garden?"

"With pleasure."

She led him through the hall and the small rear parlor where Lady Cunnington planned her days and gave orders to her servants, across the veranda bedecked with potted plants, and down the steps to the small grassy plot and the fountain in its center, which was surrounded by tall phlox, delphiniums, and sweet william. As planned, Lady Cunnington had ordered the gardener to trim the hedge at the rear of the enclosure, so Elena and Mr. Jaeger were not entirely alone.

Two wicker chairs, painted white, invited them from under the shade of the single plane tree, and

THE UNWELCOME SUITOR

Elena beckoned him to be seated there. The day was overcast and cool, but she was hot with embarrassment and chatted inconsequentially about the flowers, the tree—which her uncle had planted as a boy—and Lady Cunnington's dislike of the satyr that spouted water from his mouth in the fountain.

When she had run out of conversation, Stuart Jaeger asked again how he could serve her. He was not willing to waste words, she recalled. She was suddenly grateful for his bluntness. Perhaps, then, he wouldn't be hurt if she were equally blunt.

"I desired you to stay," she began, "because . . . I could not but conclude recently that you have rather singled me out for your attentions."

She was disturbed by the naked hope that leapt into his eyes, and she put out an instinctive hand to halt the words he seemed on the verge of uttering.

"I—I felt it only fair to tell you that . . . that my affections have long been—and still are—placed elsewhere."

The awkward moment became more awkward still during his dismayed silence. Then he tried to argue with her, to discover details, to voice suspicions of a rival. She could answer nothing concretely without giving away her widowed status, which she had promised Aunt Winifred she would not do, and so was left with no better response than to continue shaking her head. "I should cherish your friendship," she said finally, "but kindly believe that it can be no deeper than friendship."

"Am I to believe, then, that you seek only beaux and frippery, not a husband? Damme! What admirable fairness!"

She flushed under the hard stare of his clear cool eyes and bit her lip. "I cannot be more frank, forgive me. I only wished to explain because I value your regard."

Her obvious distress softened him and he grew philosophical, admitting his dreams of her were more fancy than real, that he intended to retire soon to his estate in Shropshire, disliking London, and he had known all along she was far too lovely to be buried away in the country with a rustic like himself.

Relieved, she smiled a little and tried to deny his compliments as beside the point. Then, remembering something about his interest in waterfowl, she brought in Charlotte Saxton's uncanny way with her pet birds.

"Birds!" Mr. Jaeger responded, staring off into space. "Really?" She hoped she caught a tone of interest in the exclamation; at any rate the sarcasm was now gone. Then he arose from the wicker chair and faced her. "I suspect you are trying to console me. I shan't be consoled. I shall try again. You may alter in a year or two."

She shook her head, stood, and held out her hand. He brushed it with his lips, gave her a wry smile, and departed. Elena sighed and returned to the house to find Lady Cunnington. The most difficult part of her plan had gone off as well as she could have expected. Now she must see to the second part.

"To Astley's?" Lady Cunnington asked incredulously as she checked the placement of china and silverware on the dining table. (A dozen close friends of the Cunningtons were coming to dinner.) "Oh, heavens, no! All the hoi polloi go to Astley's Circus. Wherever did you get such an idea?"

"From Charlotte. She's mad about horses as well as birds, and they are presenting a big equestrian

THE UNWELCOME SUITOR

show next week, featuring a famous family of trainers from Hungary. Surely you've seen the bills. They're all over the city."

"I never notice such things," her aunt said. "And I'm amazed you would. Or that you think you even have the time. We are scheduled up to our ears: Almack's Wednesday, the opera Thursday, the Princess de Lieven's for dinner Friday, the Saturday luncheon with Lady Jersey. And then the Carleton House invitation is only two weeks away, and we must have a new gown for you, Elena. None of yours is quite up to Court dress, and of course you can't wear your Presentation dress again. That means deciding on style and fabric, tomorrow at the latest. And more fittings, and . . ."

Elena jumped in when Lady Cunnington hesitated long enough to draw breath. "Next Tuesday, then, Aunt Winifred. I looked at my own calendar, and I'm sure it's free. I hoped we might make up a party: Charlotte and Mr. Jaeger; myself and Lord Harcourt; you and Uncle Geoffrey, which would be six and quite safe, I should think, even in Lambeth. And we could hire a special box and never rub elbows with the hoi polloi, as you call them."

Aunt Winifred continued to shake her head over the idea, then seemed struck by something Elena had said. "Lord Harcourt? Oh, Elena, really? I thought you said . . ."

"I promised to be his friend, only that."

Lady Cunnington looked skeptical, but Elena returned her gaze levelly. "Well," her aunt said, "if you really think Lord Harcourt would go to such a place. I shall need to consult Lord Cunnington, of course. Perhaps, if we add Hunter to the carriage. He's the biggest footman we have, over fifteen stone . . ." Her voice trailed off thoughtfully, and Elena decided the battle was half-won.

"And how did it go with Mr. Jaeger in the garden?" Lady Cunnington pursued. She had gone along with Elena's plan, but she had not liked it.

"I think I have convinced him I am not available. I tried to give him a gentle prod in Charlotte's direction. I hope the equestrian show will give him another."

"You should be thinking of your own suitor, Elena, not someone else's."

Elena smiled—a roguish, determined smile her aunt was not acquainted with. "Don't worry, dear Aunt, I am thinking of him."

This seemed entirely contradictory to what Elena had said before about Lord Harcourt being only a friend, and perplexed Lady Cunnington even further.

It wasn't until she tried to compose a note to Lord Harcourt the following day that Elena realized how completely she had lied—to Mr. Jaeger, to Aunt Winifred, to herself. And especially to Lord Harcourt.

He had sent her flowers, which arrived that morning—two dozen dew-fresh red roses, which Aunt Winifred had observed with raised eyebrows and a meaningful smile. His card was with them. To it he had added, "Will you be at Almack's tomorrow night?" This, following a night of sleeplessness interspersed by sensual dreams, had put Elena in a distracted haze. Rodney's sacred image was fading, however much she tried to recapture it, and it was Lord Harcourt (Lawrence, his remembered voice insisted) . . . very well, *Lawrence*, who was turning her giddy senses upside down with the feel and scent of him in her arms, her ears echoing to his voice, her

THE UNWELCOME SUITOR

vision challenged by his changeable eyes and that lean jawline that could be iron-hard or soft and vulnerable with desire . . .

Betray Rodney's love? Perhaps it wouldn't be betrayal. Certainly no one else seemed to think so. Maybe the most foolish part of her short time with Rodney was not the elopement but her conviction that the few days they had shared were enough to last a lifetime.

She feared and yet longed to see Lawrence again. She could not have even considered another man to be her escort to the outing to Astley's; yet she distrusted her own instincts. She had questioned whether he or Rodney or any of them were attracted to her for beauty's sake alone, but how did one answer such a question? Did she even have the self-discipline to devise some kind of testing when her instincts urged her to simply plunge again, willy-nilly, into the heady intoxication of love?

Now her pen remained poised above the note she intended to include in Lady Cunnington's invitation to Lord Harcourt. Lord Cunnington had, surprisingly, agreed to the outing to Astley's Circus, and once he had assented, Lady Cunnington herself had shown a tentative interest at breakfast in the equestrian show. Everything was, therefore, going according to plan, except for her present dilemma—what to write.

How was she to acknowledge the flowers, to begin with? Red roses were for lovers, and while she longed to encourage him, she didn't quite dare to. She settled, finally, upon a warm but noncommittal thank-you, and a short explanation of the invitation. At Lady Wallingham's, Mr. Jaeger had expressed admiration for Lord Harcourt's progressive political ideas, and Lawrence had briefly said something about looking into Mr. Jaeger's study of waterfowl. They both had rooms at the Clairmont and were, by now, fairly well acquainted, so he should consider it a congenial evening.

"Yes," she wrote him, "I will be at Almack's tomorrow night. I hope it won't be as nerve-racking as I have been led to believe. The roses are so lovely, and I do thank you for them. I shall keep my thoughts on them rather than on how well I do the quadrille before Lady Jersey and the Duke of Devonshire.

"The equestrian show is my idea. Do say you will go. Lady Cunnington is also inviting Mr. Stuart Jaeger and Miss Charlotte Saxton, who would make an ideal couple, if only we can convince *him* of it. I'm daring to play matchmaker and hope you will concur."

Uncle Geoffrey grumbled that Almack's was a bore. One must dress in what amounted to Court dress—breeches and hose; white neckcloth folded and starched to perfection; and on top of it all, the useless *sous bras*, the old tricorn hat, no longer worn on the head but, for some obscure reason known only to the gods of fashion, folded and tucked under one arm. He also complained about the drinks.

"No reason why they couldn't allow us poor males a drop of spirits occasionally. Makes the evening damned slow."

"Lemonade is more satisfying when one is thirsty," Lady Cunnington retorted. "And you know as well as I there are always those who don't know when they have had enough spirits. Fruit punch is indispensable to correct manners."

Elena sympathized with her uncle but dared not echo his viewpoint. She was the cause of it all, for she must have a male relative escort her and a female to chaperone her. She wore another new gown tonight, a deep-blue silk that matched her eyes. A gauzy overskirt of white muslin and lace was embroidered with blue butterflies. The shade of pale iridescent blue in the sapphires at her throat was echoed in her satin slippers, her elbow-length gloves, and the bows and brilliants the hairdresser had ingeniously fastened in her hair, which was curled in clusters over each ear.

When the ballroom opened before them, one hundred feet of it, ornately pilastered and columned, with enormous chandeliers splashing light on jewels and glistening silks and brocades, she saw Lord Harcourt almost immediately. Dressed again in severe black and white, he was dancing to the strains of an old Scottish jig. His partner was Lady Cordelia Radcliffe.

After a moment Elena recognized the sickening ache that wrenched her for what it was—sheer jealousy. A fitting lesson for her. No doubt Charlotte had felt the same on watching her dancing with Mr. Jaeger. She tried to ignore the sensation as she accompanied Lord and Lady Cunnington to pay duty to Lady Jersey, Lady Cowper, the Princess de Lieven, and Lady Sefton, four of the ladies who ruled Almack's.

As Lord Cunnington led her out for a reel, Elena kept her eyes averted from Lord Harcourt at the other end of the line and remembered her earnest (and false) plea to him that they only be friends. Perhaps he was indicating he would not accept such terms. He had not yet responded to Lady Cunnington's invitation.

However, Charlotte had, and sometime later, when they were able to greet each other, she expressed her delight at the prospect of the equestrian show. Her eyes were sparkling and her smile made her large plain features almost pretty. "However, Mama is not quite sure how respectable the atmosphere is at Astley's," she confided. "If the invitation hadn't come from Lady Cunnington, she might not have allowed it."

Elena assured her it was both proper and safe, for they would be in a group, with footmen to guard the carriage both ways and a private box at the amphitheater itself.

Her partners for the dances that followed were handpicked by Lady Cunnington or one of Almack's patronesses. She tried not to think about Lawrence's elusive presence until she was led out for a quadrille by a young man she scarcely knew, and discovered they would dance it with Lord Harcourt and Lady Cordelia. As they bowed to one another, she barely glanced at him.

Lady Cordelia was a curiously listless dancer, always somewhat lagging in the beat, smiling a bit apologetically when she missed a cue, seeming positively uncomfortable at times. Lord Harcourt was gallant and protective of his partner, but each time Elena looked at him, he was watching her and she was forced to drop her eyes. Her cheeks went hot whenever an exchange of partners forced them to touch hands. After the music ended and all had bowed again to one another, he said in a low tone, "The waltz, Miss Tyndale." Then he escorted Lady Cordelia off the floor.

Two dances later a waltz was played, and as she had half-expected, he was standing before her, taking her from the man Lady Cowper had tapped for her, explaining with a smile, "This was prearranged, Lady Cowper."

"Fie on you, Lord Harcourt," Elena reproved him

when they were safely in the middle of the floor. "You will surely be given the boot for interfering with Lady Cowper's plans."

"It was a useless evening until now. So I'll leave gladly if she boots me out. But only if you come with me." His eyes, warm and daring, teased her, bestowing upon her wings and extravagent fancies—fancies such as Rodney had once aroused in her. That memory produced a coldness about her heart.

"And what of Lady Cordelia?" she asked faintly.

"My bringing her tonight was an obligation. I'm her sole male relative."

"Only an obligation? The poor lady!"

"She doesn't care for dancing. And she never learnt the waltz and has refused to try it, so I was free to ask you." His expression was insouciant. Even as they responded to the music, his eyes were taking in her gown, her hair, and lingering on her face. "And you," he added, "you have altered marvelously since our last dance, Miss Tyndale."

"In what way?" She tilted her head, smiling at him, unable to refrain from playing up to his admiration.

"I cannot tell you here," he countered. "Perhaps I may call on you tomorrow and explain?"

Her heart lurched. "I . . . Lady Cunnington says we will be gone most of the day."

"The following day, then?"

"Perhaps. Did you receive Lady Cunnington's invitation?"

"And your note? Yes, I did. And will be delighted to accompany you to Astley's Circus."

"What think you of my matchmaking idea?"

He smiled but shook his head at her. "Such plans are rarely realized, you know."

"I'm sorry you feel that way."

"Don't be." He swung her around in an impromptu

whirl. "I don't want you to be sorry about a thing." After a pause he added, "You are incredibly lovely tonight, Elena."

She smiled back, once more floating on air, happy, for the moment, to be what he proclaimed her.

12

It was a fleeting happiness. The change was heralded the following day by a brief formal note, hand-delivered to Lady Cunnington, that read: "The Princess de Lieven regrets that, due to an illness in the family, it has been necessary to cancel the Friday-evening soiree to which you were invited."

The Princess, wife of the Russian ambassador, was one of London's most popular and talked-about hostesses. Though deploring the cancelation, Lady Cunnington thought little of it and sent back a note of sympathy. She nearly forgot to tell Elena until they had returned from the dressmaker's late in the afternoon. Then, after she had ordered a hasty tea—all the meal they would have time for before dressing for the opera—she mentioned the situation.

"It is no great matter," she said comfortably. "Doubtless there will be a later invitation to make it up." She led the way into the parlor and, as Elena sat in her usual chair in front of the tea table, began to inspect the furniture with her forefinger for signs of dust—a ritual she performed every day on at least one room to keep the maids on their toes.

After the girl had brought in the tea service with a tray of cucumber sandwiches and scones, Elena said,

"From what I've heard of the Princess, I don't really mind, Aunt Winifred."

"That's neither here nor there, child. One doesn't see that much of the hostess at a function like this, anyway, unless one is a special friend. What *is* important is all the other people who will be there..." She broke off to take a bite of sandwich, and just then Ross appeared with another hand-delivered letter. It was from Lady Jersey, who had invited them for Saturday luncheon. Lady Cunnington put down her sandwich, broke the seal, and scanned the sheet to see if it bore reading aloud.

Elena watched expectantly and was surprised at the frown that grew in her aunt's forehead.

"What is it, Aunt?" she asked.

"It's beyond belief," Lady Cunnington muttered. "Whoever..." She took a deep breath and gazed at Elena severely. "I trust you haven't let the cat out of the bag concerning your elopement."

"No, indeed, I only told Mr. Jaeger what we agreed I might—that my affections were elsewhere. It was difficult, for he quizzed me, but I don't collect I gave any hint. What *is* it, Aunt Winifred?"

"Well, I doubt very much Mr. Jaeger is responsible. But someone is. A rumor, my dear, which, unhappily, has an element of truth but has been viciously distorted." She perused the letter again. "I daresay I may as well read you the whole of it. 'My dear Winifred,' it begins. Lady Jersey and I are not close, understand, so I feel she does tend to overdo the familiarity. 'I regret I must withdraw my invitation to you and Miss Tyndale for Saturday next. Since we have known each other a number of years, I feel an explanation is due you. I have heard, from what I consider an impeccable source, that Miss Tyndale is appearing in Society under false pretenses. That last September she eloped to Gretna Green with a young officer of questionable character, who abandoned her and returned to his regiment on the Continent after a few days. After being deserted, Miss Tyndale retired to the country, not only in grief but because she was *enceinte* with this man's love-child. The family hushed up the whole episode and denied any such liaison had occurred, their infamous suppression of the truth made easier when the child was stillborn.

" 'I needn't tell you the seriousness of this charge, inasmuch as Miss Tyndale has had the temerity to be presented to the Queen as a young lady of irreproachable reputation and has been likewise presented at Almack's, drawing great admiration from everyone, but especially from many men of high rank, because of her beauty and bearing.

" 'You ought to know as well as anyone, my dear Winifred, that beauty cannot be the excuse for such a crime. I am most disappointed to find you sponsoring a relative of such blemished character, for it cannot help but reflect on your own reputation. I could not now consider introducing Miss Tyndale to any of the young ladies that I have invited to my Saturday affair.

" 'I remain, Madame,

" 'Yours obligingly, etc., etc.,
Sarah Sophia Child, Countess of Jersey.'

"There—you see?" Aunt Winifred's frame shook with rage. "She doesn't even give us a chance to explain or deny or verify! She lacks even the decency to name your accuser. It is monstrous!"

Blood had rushed to Elena's head at the sentence accusing Rodney of having a "questionable character." As the charges grew worse, the familiar parlor swayed and almost passed from view. She closed her eyes with a shudder.

"Elena," Aunt Winifred said in a commanding voice. "There was, definitely, a wedding?"

"Yes," Elena whispered.

"Before you consummated . . . ?"

Elena opened her eyes in surprise. "Does it matter?" she asked bitterly. "Does any of it matter now?"

"I want to know."

"It took us some days to arrive at Gretna Green. Another day to arrange the ceremony. Rodney wanted . . ." She faltered before her aunt's scrutiny. "I—I insisted on separate rooms," she finished, "until after the ceremony."

Aunt Winifred relaxed her glare only a little. "And were you, as she accused, with child?"

"No, I never was."

Lady Cunnington gave a large sigh. "I didn't think Theresa would fib me about so important a thing. Then we can deny it utterly. I shall write Lady Jersey and demand to know just what her 'impeccable source' is."

"No, Aunt, pray do not."

"Why ever not? If Lady Jersey knows, so may many others . . . Heavens! The Princess de Lieven . . ." Her voice broke off, stricken.

"Probably was withdrawing her invitation for the same reason," Elena finished for her. "If Lady Jersey knows, everyone else does, too. But I don't care a pin. I never thought of myself as eligible, anyway."

"What about Lord Harcourt?" Lady Cunnington asked.

Elena bit her lip to counteract a sudden pounding

in her temples. "It doesn't matter," she insisted. "Now I can go home, which is what I wanted to do anyway."

"Nonsense. Have you no fighting spirit? We must sink this thing."

Elena hadn't the heart to argue, nor did she have the time right then. Lady Cunnington looked at the mantel clock and exclaimed at the time, and urged Elena to at least drink the tea if she could not manage the food. They must appear at the opera in spite of the letter. Somehow they would prove Lady Jersey and her "impeccable source" quite wrong.

The arrival of three more letters, also canceling future invitations with varying degrees of evasiveness, did not change her mind. But there was no triumph for them at the opera. When, during the intermission between the acts of Gluck's *Orfeo*, Lady Cunnington attempted to introduce Elena to two couples she knew, she was cut dead. On the way home she was unbowed but thoughtful. Elena, having spent the longest evening of her life in anguished embarrassment, was relieved by her silence.

The following day other cancelations arrived, including the invitation to Carleton House. Although this brought on a storm of protest from her aunt and a call to her maid for the hartshorn, Elena tried hard to ignore the mail until a letter was delivered to her from Lord Harcourt.

> I have been called to Penton Hill because of an emergency. One of my most trusted servants has been taken ill and is, it seems, at death's door. I know you will understand my obligation to attend him. I shall try to return in time to call

on you Sunday next. Tuesday evening without fail.

> Your devoted,
> Lawrence

He had written it hurriedly and she had no reason to suspect it was anything but sincere; yet its very brevity, without a salutation, chilled her. She did not show it to Lady Cunnington, who seemed more and more distraught each time the door knocker sounded. By the time they usually left for their calling rounds, the Baroness had refused to look at any more messages. At last she canceled her order to have the carriage brought around. "We'll have a rousing game of backgammon," she said with false briskness. "Or do you prefer piquet? I have not had a relaxing afternoon for weeks. It will be a welcome change."

Elena felt she had been plunged into a kind of limbo. If it hadn't been for the prospect of the equestrian show the following Tuesday, she would have pleaded for a return to Tyndale Green immediately. Now, attending the show seemed important not only to her plan for furthering a romance between Mr. Jaeger and Charlotte, but as relief from the wounds inflicted on her by all those canceled invitations. She had maintained she didn't care, but that wasn't true, after all. At Astley's Circus in Lambeth she could enjoy herself and, since no one they knew was likely to encounter them, not run the risk of an embarrassing cut.

On Sunday afternoon Lady Cunnington, having received no answer to her letter to Lady Jersey asking that she name the source of the rumor, ordered the coach. She insisted Elena accompany her and instructed the coachman to drive them to Berkeley Square, where Lady Jersey lived.

Lady Jersey refused to receive them. So did the other ladies they afterward called upon.

"This is beyond belief," Lady Cunnington muttered between her teeth as the last message, "Lady Cowper is not at home this afternoon," was delivered to her. "One would think we had some contagious disease."

Elena, her soft chin set, said nothing.

Lord Harcourt did not appear that day, and on Monday Elena received a note from Charlotte. The linen was blotted with watermarks that looked suspiciously like tears. She tore open the seal hastily.

Dearest Elena,

Mama insists I write you to break our engagement for Tuesday night. I have been arguing with her as long and hard as I dare, but it is like addressing a stone. She will not be moved. It is not because of Astley's *per se* (although she did not like our going there), but because of a rumor she had heard about *you*. I told her to disbelieve it, for I'd go bail that if any of it were true you would have told me. I won't repeat the details—you know them, I am sure, for Lady Jersey said Saturday she had written Lady Cunnington concerning it.

I'm most dreadfully sorry. If it were up to me, I would pay no attention, for I think it the most bird-witted *fudge*. But Mama . . .

I pray you let me know your plans. Although Mama will not allow me to see you for the present (as though I might somehow be contaminated—what rubbish!) things *must* change. And I wish you to know *I* trust you and love you.

As ever,
Charlotte

Elena showed the letter to Lady Cunnington as soon as she had wiped away her own unexpected tears. Like a drowning person who can think of nothing but to arrive on solid ground and breathe fresh air again, she longed for the haven of Tyndale Green.

"There is no sense in my staying in London, Aunt Winifred. My last reason is gone—and now I shall never know if I might have brought Charlotte and Mr. Jaeger together or not. I pray you, allow me to go home tomorrow. And forgive me for bringing all this censure down on your head."

"There is nothing to forgive, child," Aunt Winifred said gruffly. "I knew what I was about." She reached out and gathered her niece to her bosom. Elena burst into more tears.

"There, there, my dear. We could still fight it, you know. I have thought I might write up a retraction and publish it in the *Morning Post*."

"Oh, no, Aunt Winifred, I just want to go home," Elena wailed.

Absently her aunt patted her back. "Very well, very well. I daresay it will all die down in time, anyway. It always does. But what a shame to have all our beautiful plans end so horribly."

"I am only worried about what to tell Mama and Papa," Elena confessed, backing away from her aunt's embrace and reaching into her skirt pocket for her handkerchief.

"Well, now . . ." Lady Cunnington thought a

minute. "The truth, of course. But you will need some support, won't you. I believe I shall come along. It's been a while since I've seen my sister, and Geoffrey can do nicely without me for a few days."

13

"Elena! Winifred! Why didn't you let us know you were coming? Whatever has happened?"

Lady Theresa tried to hide it with a hug and a peck on her cheek, but Elena knew her mother was more disturbed than happy at their unexpected appearance. They had arrived late in the afternoon as Lady Theresa and Sir John were enjoying tea on the lawn, under the shade of the large copper beech that was her father's pride. She and Lady Cunnington had been up before dawn, supervising the packing. The trunks would arrive later, in the wagon. Elena hardly knew how to reply to her mother. The nine-hour journey had been tiresome and hot, although dry roads had helped accomplish it with a minimum of delay, and her thoughts were chaotic and downhearted.

She was grateful when Winifred answered for her. "Do allow us to freshen up and then we'll explain. I apologize for barging in on you this way, but Elena is simply coming home, and you needn't put on the dog for me, Theresa, I'm your sister."

Sir John rose and hugged his daughter and said it was good to have her home. Comforted by his

THE UNWELCOME SUITOR

unquestioning devotion, she returned his hug mutely, then followed Jane upstairs to her room. If her father had been the only one to tell, she might have done so at once.

She dallied in her room after washing and changing into an old afternoon dress of green sprigged muslin, reluctant to face her mother's questions, which would demand countless details and endless review. She looked out her window in satisfaction at the slope of smooth, recently cut and rolled lawn, at the tall oaks and chestnuts, the sheep grazing in the distance, the dovecotes on their high poles where the inhabitants fluttered endlessly in and out of their holes, feathers shimmering blue and magenta and silver in the sunlight. If only she could simply enjoy all this peace and beauty without explaining, or even thinking about, all that had occurred.

But hunger finally demanded that she delay no longer, and she descended the long, curved stairway and went out a side door to the knoll where Aunt Winifred had already settled with her parents in the outdoor cane chairs. Lady Theresa, shorter than Lady Cunnington but quite as stout, with hair she had kept dark with a brown dye, poured tea. Her plump white hands, ringed with her favorite opals and diamonds, were graceful and efficient.

Sir John was accepting a second cup from his wife. His gray hair receded from a generous forehead, but his lined features and deep blue eyes, which Elena had inherited, were still handsome. He had kept his tall frame trim despite an otherwise sedentary life with much walking and a strict two-meal-a-day diet, after which he never drank any spirits beyond a small glass of claret or sherry.

Elena kissed her mother and father on the forehead in turn and received from Sir John a long, searching look that tried to divine her state of mind. She smiled at him with tremulous lips.

"Winifred has told us all about it," Lady Theresa said, handing Elena a cup of tea. "So you needn't give an account. It is most distressing. I cannot think who would have started such gossip."

"Someone who had been at Cheltenham last autumn and recognized Elena," Lady Cunnington guessed. "And, of course, there had been rumors, even then. You said so yourself."

"They had been entirely refuted, entirely," Lady Theresa asserted.

"But someone saw fit to start them again. Someone who deliberately muddled a kind of truth with malicious distortions."

"It doesn't matter," Elena said.

"Foolish girl," her mother chided. "Of course it matters. Your whole future . . ."

"Perhaps Elena is right," Sir John cut in. "Gossip always dies down with time. Now she has left London, the tongues will wag about someone more visible. You did right to come home, my dear."

"Men are so insensitive to these things," his wife put in.

"In two weeks London Society will have forgotten all about it," he reiterated mildly.

"How can you be so sure? And so calm? Your daughter's *virtue* is under attack. Her whole reputation!"

The rest of the afternoon was like that. Elena sipped her tea with a dry throat, tried not to care, and said little, except when Lady Theresa seemed inclined to blame her sister for the decision to retreat to the country.

"Aunt Winifred has been splendid," Elena

defended. "And it was my idea to come home, Mama dearest. I had been longing to do so."

"I am glad to see you, of course," her mother said, "but it does incommode the servants. We are expecting the Duke and Duchess of Malvern today or tomorrow. They are journeying home to Lincoln from Bath. The Duchess thinks the waters at Bath much superior to those at Cheltenham for her vapors. It is a pity they did not take you *there* last autumn."

Never, Elena thought, would she be allowed to forget what happened last autumn. Always, memories would haunt her, people like the Duke and Duchess would remind her, gossip would hound her. Maybe that was what she had feared about going to London —this invasion of her shining love, her first passion, by the suspicious, demeaning opinions of the world.

And Lawrence. She had left London without a word of explanation, and tonight he would wonder why. Would she ever know if he could have been the one to erase the sense of purposelessness that had descended on her? Last week's brief euphoria and the lovely waltz with him at Almack's seemed far away.

The Duke and Duchess did not come that evening. The four of them settled in for a game of whist, at which Elena's father was expert. When he and Elena, who was his partner, were not scooping up the winnings of small change that were bet on each hand, he kept them amused with droll stories of his embassy days and his contacts with those sly diplomatic warriors, Metternich, Talleyrand, and Castlereagh. He told Elena before bidding her good-night that the unusual run of hot dry weather had improved his lung condition immensely.

Elena awoke before dawn on Wednesday and remained sleepless in spite of the closed shutters and drawn bed curtains that kept out the early gray light. Feeling smothered, she rose and rang for Jane. "Tell Eliot to have Tim saddle my mare," she ordered. "I'm going riding."

"No one is up yet, mum."

"So much the better."

"An' you'd be goin' by yourself?" Jane's disapproval was obvious.

Elena was annoyed but chose to ignore it. "Yes, by myself. I shall surely be home by nine. But I cannot abide this room another minute." She struggled alone into her shift and petticoat as Jane stood mutely by as though deciding whether she should assist in such outlandish proceedings.

Finally Elena said, "Did you unpack my riding habit?"

"Yes, mum."

"Well, fetch it, then, and help me. And don't you dare rouse anyone in the house. I'll take Tim with me."

But she didn't.

She mounted her mare, a burnished brown-black five-year-old named Dark Comet, and took the path across the sheep pasture west—an unconscious choice, she thought at the time. Afterward she realized that the vision of Penton Hill, six miles to the west, had been in her mind.

Penton Hill was much larger than Tyndale Green. Its manor house, set within a thousand-acre park, was as large and ornate as a palace. The walls sprawled out in six directions on a commanding rise, with a stone facade that glinted pink in an early-morning or late-afternoon sun. Elena had been there only once when, soon after they had returned from Vienna to take up residence at Tyndale Green, she

THE UNWELCOME SUITOR

and her parents had paid a duty call on the old Viscount. She had been at once awed, charmed, and saddened by the place: awed by its size and age and the number of its servants; charmed by its enclosed courtyards and medieval-appearing pediments; saddened by the obvious neglect that had left paint to peel, window hangings to lie dirty and faded, and priceless carpets to become stained and threadbare. She had heard that the new Lord Harcourt had stirred things up a bit—servants who did not earn their keep had been replaced, repairs were being made, renovations planned. Even if she hadn't known him, she would have been curious about the changes he had wrought and what further ones he contemplated.

It would be another hot day, but now, with the sun only a bright promise on the eastern horizon, a fresh cool breeze stirred wisps of hair about her ears and forehead, clearing the dark corners from her mind, and dew sparkled gemlike on each leaf and blade of grass. The recently shorn sheep, awkward and naked without their woolly coats, ambled away from her approach or simply regarded her with dull suspicion. She urged her horse to gather speed and put it to a gallop in time to clear the hedgerow. Exhilarated by her perfect jump, she took the narrow tree-lined lane beyond at a trot.

She had left the boundary of Tyndale Green when she saw him coming toward her astride Starlight, head bare and shining with copper lights as it had on the day they first met. After her heart's first irrepressible bound of joy, she slowed the horse and proceeded toward him nervously, her lips slightly parted, ready to give a greeting that would not seem too jubilant.

"Elena!" His voice echoed toward her as soon as she was in earshot. "You're *here?*"

She waited to answer until after they had met and stopped their horses beside each other in the narrow dusty lane. "Yes." She smiled a little warily. "And you hadn't returned to London?"

"My servant, Justin, died last night—well, really, today, in the early-morning hours."

"I'm so sorry."

"He was my father's body servant and, later, mine, before I was in the Army. He was like a second father to me when I was growing up. I'm afraid his death was rather painful. I've only just left his widow." He hesitated, looking at her questioningly. "What happened to Astley's Circus? I had sent a messenger to tell you I wouldn't be back in London in time after all."

"Lady Cunnington and I arrived yesterday afternoon." She gave him a short, bitter smile. "The outing was canceled, in any case. If—if you are only riding and have no business, I'll tell you about it."

"Yes, pray do. I was just clearing my head, after being up all night. Shall we go this way?" He indicated a footpath that meandered away to her left. She followed him through an opening in the trees and then between a field of corn and a pasture. When she was able to walk her horse abreast of his, she told him the events of the past few days. "I simply had to come home," she finished.

"How terrible for you." His eyes were warm with compassion.

She shook her head, dismissing the whole situation, which already seemed less devastating now she had told it to him. "Oh, I shall mend. It is really harder on Lady Cunnington and my mother." She hesitated, but the look in his eyes urged her to imprudent confession. "Do you know, I realize now

THE UNWELCOME SUITOR

the only person I could tell this to—the only one I wished to tell—was you?"

"Thank you."

"Because I guessed it wouldn't signify to you." When he didn't reply, she added quickly. "Does it?"

"You know the answer to that. There is nothing anyone could say that would change my sentiments about you."

A pulse beat in her throat. She was forced to look away from his gaze. "You must think me terribly forward," she murmured.

"Not at all." He brought his horse too close, and Dark Comet shied and broke away. After she had brought the mare under control, he called after her, "Let me show you a place I love at Penton Hill."

"I should like that," she agreed, and waited for him to lead the way. As he passed her, the pulse began again and would not be stilled. It throbbed all through her now—in her fingers until they could hardly hold the reins, in her aching chest, and most strongly, most disturbingly, in the pit of her stomach, unexpectedly arousing her with the memory of a man's urgent body poised above her.

Rodney's body. But Rodney's face had changed, once, in an old dream, to the face of Lawrence MacLean. Like a prediction—or a warning. Careful, she told herself. He must not suspect. Yet she thought that if he so much as looked at her, he would see the very blood pounding through her veins.

And where was he taking her?

They had left the fields behind, crossed a wooded ravine overgrown with brush and summer flowers, continued into a forest of pine and larch where the path gave way to a needle-laden floor many seasons old and the scent of evergreen was pungent, fresh, nearly overwhelming. When they came out of it into a meadow carpeted with daisies, he looked back and smiled. "The infinite variety of Penton Hill. Does it please you?"

She nodded, speechless. But the best came as they climbed an overreach that ended in a small white-columned, open-sided pavilion positioned to turn the viewer's eye to a wide circle of blue lake less than a quarter-mile away. Beyond the lake sprawled Penton Hill's lovely mansion house, blushing in the newly risen sun.

"It's magnificent," she said after a long moment, her voice husky.

"It comes with me," he said. "Will you have us?"

Her eyes flew back to his. Could so casual a sentence be a proposal of marriage?

His gaze was warm as he reached out a hand to touch hers briefly. Then he dismounted and tied Starlight's reins around one of the weathered columns.

"Doubtless your horse needs a rest, too," he suggested, returning to her side.

It was her chance to thank him for showing her the view, graciously decline his offer to dismount, and take her leave. She dismissed the idea even as she considered it and instead slid off the horse into his waiting arms. When he made no move to release her, she said, with as much practicality in her tone as she could muster, "Only for a minute. Then I must r-return." And wondered if he had noticed the quaver in her voice.

He tried to search her eyes, but she avoided his—so luminous and tender—and at last he let her go, then secured Dark Comet's reins at an adjoining pillar. She walked to the edge of the pavilion, pretending to peruse the scene but really aware only of

THE UNWELCOME SUITOR

his presence behind her—the absolute danger of his presence, so that she didn't know if it would be better to appear to ignore him or turn to face him.

She hadn't much warning—just her name, uttered in little more than a whisper—before her shoulders were seized and she was turned into his arms. All her resolute resistance shattered at his touch. Their cheeks met—his warm and rough with new-beard growth; then their lips sought simultaneous contact. Her arms lifted and encircled his neck in answer to the increasing pressure of his about her ribs and waist. Her closed eyes shut out all sensations except the ever-rising pulse within her and the driving need to meld her body to his.

He withdrew slightly and turned, slid one arm up to her shoulder, and whispered, "Come." Her body responded to his as though he owned it when he brought her down to sit beside him on the wide stones edging the ravaged pavilion floor. She stared at the view steadfastly, suddenly shy of his gaze, more than ever aware of his arm about her shoulder.

"Elena."

She waited for him to continue. He did not, and she realized his silence was purposeful—to draw from her the admission he wanted without his even asking for it. She spoke, trying to still the throb that devastated her throat. "I—I shouldn't be out here alone. My family will expect . . ."

"You're not alone." A hint of laughter colored his voice. His arm tightened and she felt herself suddenly brought backward, still within the sanctuary of his arm, until she was lying prone on the ground and his face hovered only inches above hers, his eyes full of devilment.

"There. A much better position for kissing." His lips found hers again, more demanding this time, harsh and sweet at the same time, pulverizing her senses into submission. His free hand caressed her cheek, her hair, her neck, and began—inevitably, as though obeying her most secret wish—to find the buttons that fastened the snowy lace about the collar of her riding habit. She felt him (mentally helping) unfasten one button, then two, until he could bury his face in the smooth hollow at the base of her throat. With an effort she held herself still, not responding. When the intensity of her need became unbearable, she pushed him away with a little moan.

Surprised, he raised his head. His hands slipped reluctantly along the length of her arms until they gripped only her hands. "I've reached you, haven't I?" His eyes bore into hers, glittering saffron lights, demanding the truth. "At last. You cannot deny it."

"No, but . . . it's too frightening."

"Elena." Bewilderment quenched his exultation. He moved slightly away, sitting erect, and allowed her hands their freedom. Yet their gazes held each other as though at opposing ends of an invisible cord, pulled unbearably taut, yet unbreakable.

"What frightens you?" he asked softly. "Is it myself? For there's no need. I would never . . ." His questioning grew wordless, apparent only in his eyes. She knew what he was asking. Did Farnsworth force himself on you? Did you marry out of necessity? Don't you know I'm not like that?

"No." She shook her head violently. "Not you. It's . . . the way *I* feel." Her voice died out, alarmed at her own confession.

"You still dare not acknowledge that you can love another, is that it?" He seemed half-angry, retreating still further.

She shook her head again, long past such quibbling. "I—not that. Not that at all. You . . ." She

THE UNWELCOME SUITOR 147

swallowed, then finally whispered. "You've won."

She thought she had made herself clear, had acknowledged not only her abandonment of the old love but the birth of the new, and that it was a love compounded of so many things, but right now the chief manifestation was a yearning she could barely contain.

But he only repeated, "Won?" as though puzzled.

Her face relaxed; it was no longer wary and guarded, and a smile invaded her lips. He leaned over her again, recaptured her hands, and repeated, "Won?" with growing understanding.

She laughed. "Don't be a featherhead. I know you take my meaning."

"You must tell it to me."

"I cannot. You must ask me first."

"So . . . you admit it is possible, after all, to love more than one man in a lifetime?" he asked cautiously.

She nodded quickly, breathing hard.

"You reject your pledge that you will never marry again?"

"I— 'Twas not a pledge, exactly."

"Your notion, then. Your ridiculous, woolly-crowned notion." He pulled her into his arms, cradling her and rocking her back and forth as though she were a child, his cheek against her hair. "I think I'm dreaming. I'm light-headed from being up all night, and it's a dream, a fantasy. You'll evaporate with the dew in the new day's sun . . ."

"If so, then I'm dreaming, too."

He lifted his head suddenly and traced with gentle fingers the line of her cheekbone down to her chin. "Lovely, lovely Elena. How real you look—and feel. But tell me. Prove to me it's real. Do you really love me, after all your parrying and evasion?"

"I love you." Her voice was steadfast. It was suddenly an easy thing to say.

"And you will marry me?"

"I thought you would never come to the point." Her smile deepened, admitting a dimple to the corner of her mouth.

"Today? Tomorrow? Next week? I confess, now I have you in my arms I don't want to let you go, not even for a moment." His lips brushed her forehead and she was enveloped again in his kisses, which sought every angle and plane of her face and throat, arousing the wild desire that she had hidden by her banter.

Finally she managed to draw away from him, laughing. "My Lord!"

"Lawrence." His eyebrows drew together in a ferocious frown. "What, are you a serving wench that you should address me 'my Lord'?"

"Then pray do not use me as you would a serving wench. Or do you not crave an answer to your question, after all?"

"I crave it," he said, suddenly sober. "Speak, my lady."

"You must ask my father, of course. But I see no obstacle there."

"Very well." He kissed her upturned nose lightly. "I shall call on him as soon as I can. It will have to wait until this evening. Justin's funeral will be this afternoon. Much needs to be arranged and I will be expected to say a few words at the gravesite."

"Perhaps you should wait until tomorrow morning. We are expecting the Duke and Duchess of Malvern, and everything will be at sevenses the rest of today."

"You are putting me off again, I see."

"Lawrence!" She spoke his name with a new freedom that amazed her. "Never. I only want it to be just right. I want it to be . . . the first consideration, and it might not be so if you came tonight. And then there is your mother. She will object."

"The plague take my mother."

"No, you mustn't speak so." Elena reached up a tender chiding hand to his cheek. "We must have her blessing, too. I want everything to be quite perfect. It's very important to me."

"Then we shall have it, though the devil only knows how."

She smiled and smoothed away the frown in his forehead with her fingertips, confident he could overcome whatever obstacle still remained in their path. "And now I really must take myself off." She rose and he jumped to his feet beside her, retaining his hold on her hand. "You *will* come tomorrow morning?" she asked.

"Without fail. I promise."

She thought she couldn't bear to be parted from him. But once they had managed it, she directed Dark Comet home with singing in her heart.

14

Lady Theresa, having been visited by the Malverns' outrider with news that the Duke and Duchess would soon arrive, was too distracted to pay much attention to how late Elena arrived at the breakfast table. She had already left it and was going over details with her cook for the noon meal before her daughter returned. She emphasized that the food and service must be impeccable for as long as the Duke and Duchess chose to stay.

The previous autumn the Duke, full of his family's long connection with the royal household at Windsor, had seemed to look down his long nose at the Tyndales' humbler establishment and had even ventured to advise Lady Theresa as to the manner of her table settings. Having planned dinners for a number of great persons in Vienna, Lady Theresa had been secretly vexed. She was determined there should be no cause for his Grace's unwanted advice this time. As she had told her husband, the strain on one's nerves would scarcely have been worth the visit of a top-lofty aristocrat like the Duke had not the Duchess been one of her oldest and dearest friends.

Elena was just congratulating herself on not

THE UNWELCOME SUITOR 151

having encountered her mother on the way to her room when she was met instead by Lady Cunnington in the hallway. Aunt Winifred fixed on her a questioning stare and said, "Jane said you had gone off. You seem to have acquired a taste for early-morning rides."

Elena felt her cheeks go hot. "I couldn't sleep." She saw her aunt's eyes fix on her hair, several strands of which had come unpinned during Lawrence's embraces. "I—I did meet Lord Harcourt, also out riding," she confessed. "He had been abroad all night. His servant died before dawn. The funeral is this afternoon." As her aunt waited, expecting more, she went on hesitantly, "I . . . we rode together for a while and talked. We lost track of the time."

"And you have apparently also lost your dislike of him."

Lady Cunnington's tone was dry, her face unsmiling, but Elena caught the twinkle in her eye and her own smile broke through irresistibly. "You might say that," she admitted, and escaped upstairs to bathe and change her clothes, not quite sure why she didn't spill out the whole truth at once.

Jane, taking care of her clothes, noticed smudges of dirt on the back of her riding habit and, of course, mentioned it.

"Don't give me one of your scolds, Jane," Elena retorted. "I am far too happy to bother with such trifles. Lord Harcourt has asked me to marry him."

"Oh, mum!" Jane's eyes went round with delight. "Then you'll be Lady Harcourt?"

"I believe that's the way it works."

"An' live at Penton Hill?"

"Yes, indeed. Would you like to live there?"

Jane admitted to a lifelong ambition to merely see the inside of the mansion. Elena laughed and assured her she would, perhaps, end up seeing more of it than she would want. Then she brought her maid back to earth by saying, "Now, Jane, you must not speak of this to any of the other servants until Lord Harcourt has spoken to Papa."

"Oh, no, mum!"

"You must promise that you will not," Elena insisted, suddenly wishing she had said nothing—yet she had needed to tell someone. Jane solemnly promised.

The Malverns arrived at noon, their splendid berlin and four matched roans driven by a perspiring coachman smothered in wig, cocked hat, and plush breeches. They were accompanied by two liveried footmen riding postilion and followed by two more vehicles for servants and luggage.

The Duchess of Malvern had never allowed her own superior social position and wealth to interfere with her childhood friendship for Lady Theresa. Childless herself, she had been so taken with Elena at sixteen that she had jokingly offered to adopt her. When her good offices in chaperoning Elena to Cheltenham had ended in the disastrous elopement with her own nephew, the Duchess had been quite overcome with mortification. She could not, of course, have been considered responsible for Captain Farnsworth's scandalous conduct, she had been quick to point out, for she had barely known him. He was the son of a younger brother she hadn't seen for years, and their meeting in Cheltenham had been entirely by chance. It had been the nephew's own importunities that had led her to introduce Elena to him, and since he was presentable and properly grateful for any favor shown him, the Duchess had thought there was little harm in him.

"Little did we know, my dear!" she had said to

THE UNWELCOME SUITOR 153

Lady Theresa and Sir John after it was all over. "We knew absolutely nothing of Rodney except for the fact of his Army career since he had reached maturity. I should have inquired—I shall never forgive myself for that—but one expects one's own nephew to act the gentleman, after all."

To Lady Theresa's annoyance, her friend seemed bent on repeating her regrets all over again when, about midafternoon, with the Duke viewing the construction of new garden terraces with Sir John, the two friends and Lady Cunnington were engaged in needlework and conversation in the cool north parlor.

"It is all over and done with," Lady Theresa said, hoping to stem a further review of the disaster, which, she feared, now seemed doomed to never-ending repercussions.

"And is Elena totally recovered, then? She did look blooming at table—especially lovely in that blue muslin. But I noticed she scarce ate a thing."

Lady Theresa and her sister exchanged glances. "She had a late breakfast," Elena's mother said.

"A short visit home, is it?" the Duchess pursued. "I had understood she was in London for the Season."

"Indeed, she has been," Lady Cunnington put in. "But Elena had become quite worn out with all our racketing about Town, and needed a short rest."

"Any prospects?" asked Lady Theresa's indefatigable friend.

"Not at the moment," Lady Theresa began, while Winifred began, "Actually . . ."

Again their eyes met. " . . . there *is* a young man," Lady Cunnington continued. "Lord Harcourt."

"Our new neighbor!" Lady Theresa exclaimed with pleasure. "Oh, how splendid."

"We mustn't, of course, count our chickens," Lady

Cunnington cautioned. "But he is assuredly interested."

"And Elena?"

"Not . . . disinterested," Lady Cunnington admitted with satisfaction.

"I am delighted," the Duchess said. "For we have discovered something quite shocking about Rodney. I had hesitated to tell you, for fear it would fret Elena even more, but if she is fully recovered . . ."

"What is it?" Lady Theresa asked, as she hesitated.

"Well, of course, one mislikes to speak ill of the dead, but *that man* . . ."

She stopped abruptly as Elena, having found a long abandoned piece of embroidery work with which to occupy her hands, entered the parlor from the hall.

"Speak ill of whom?" Elena asked innocently as she sat near her mother. "Pardon my interrupting, ma'am." All three women looked aghast, as though they had been caught swearing like fishwives. Elena looked from one to the other in growing astonishment. "I'm sorry, but . . . What *is* it?"

Lady Cunnington recovered first. "Well, she is not, after all, a child," she said. "Elena, my dear, I mean you. I think you can stand to hear whatever it is. Perhaps it would even be good if you did."

"Hear what?" Elena asked with foreboding.

"Something about Captain Farnsworth," her mother rushed in. "Yes, Genevieve, I agree with Winifred. She may as well hear it, too. And now you have gone this far, I shall never rest until you inform *me*."

"Very well." But the Duchess looked nonplussed for a long moment. "It is *very* shocking," she repeated. The others only waited for her to continue.

THE UNWELCOME SUITOR 155

"We—the Duke and I—have learned that Rodney was previously married, in Portugal."

Elena, who had frozen at the mention of Rodney's name, now went white. "Married?" she repeated faintly.

"Yes, indeed, *married*. And to a Portuguese peasant," the Duchess said dramatically. "She was not even a lady."

Having caught their attention completely—every needle waited, quiet in its owner's hand—the Duchess lowered her voice and continued. "It was most singular. She found us in Bath no more than five weeks ago. This particular morning she sent word by some grubby urchin that a 'Ma*dame* Farnsworth' wished to see his Grace. Well, we thought it might be my younger brother's wife. She is part French and has never been able to keep decent servants. But I thought it curious, for I supposed them to be in Italy. However, I consulted the Duke, and we invited her to come that afternoon. We even received her in the formal parlor. She turned out to be a very common woman, dressed all in black homespun. Imagine our shock to see that she had a *child* with her." Her eyes moved to Elena. "A boy about three. She spoke very poor English, but she continually pointed to the boy and said, 'Capitaõ Farnsworth's *son*.' "

"They were really married?" Lady Theresa asked.

"Indeed they were. She had brought a document to prove it. Married in a Roman church, my dears, by a priest. The document was duly signed by the priest and some official of the village. I'd never heard of the place. The Duke had the certificate verified because she was asking, believe it or not, for her rights as his widow, as the mother of his son. She had heard somehow of Rodney's death and had come all that distance to claim the child's inheritance. She kept telling the Duke in her broken English that she knew she had married 'veree great gentlemans,' and of course she supposed there was money to be had."

"What on earth did you do with her?" Lady Cunnington asked.

"Well, my dears, we finally found an Army colonel who spoke good Portuguese and he translated for us. It seems she had no money left, for it had taken all she could muster just to make the journey. Poor Freddie, Rodney's father, has been dead for several years, and my other brother, as I say, is in Italy, but this woman had been able somehow to trace me as Rodney's relative and dump her request into our laps. She expected to be made rich." She shook her head at the foolishness of such an idea.

"Of course we had to tell her that Captain Farnsworth had left no money to speak of. What remained at his death had gone to pay off the most appalling gambling debts. So many young officers—and gentlemen in general—gamble far too much, don't you think? But there was nothing left for her, nothing." The Duchess gave a huge sigh and fell silent.

Elena's initial shock had given way to numbness, followed by a sense of unreality. This could not be Rodney the Duchess spoke of, *her* Rodney, married to a peasant woman, father of her son, and an extravagant, irresponsible gambler to boot. She had known he gambled at Cheltenham, but so did all the other officers and fashionable ladies and gentlemen. It was a way to pass the time. It had never occurred to her he had bet away his entire living. And the poor woman . . .

"What did she do, then?" Elena asked, startling her mother, who was regarding her anxiously,

THE UNWELCOME SUITOR 157

expecting her to burst into tears. "This Portuguese woman. Where has she gone?"

"I really have no idea," the Duchess answered. "We did give her some money—enough for a hotel room for a few nights and passage home for her and the child. She was enormously grateful, of course, but she made no further effort to contact us. I must say she showed civility in that. When the Duke checked at the hotel, as we were preparing to come on home, he learned she had left soon after his last interview with her. There was, really, nothing more to be done."

"I daresay she has returned to Portugal, then," Lady Theresa said as a way of comforting Elena. "You were kindness itself. The poor woman could not have expected more."

"All for the best, of course," Lady Cunnington put in. "But how terrible it would have been for Elena had the Captain lived!"

"I was never really married to him, then, was I?" Elena said softly, in a tone of discovery. She was staring at the floor, seeing nothing.

"No, dear," the Duchess of Malvern said kindly. "You were dreadfully deceived, and I am as sorry as can be that someone of my own family should have . . ."

"All that fuss about a clergyman," Elena broke in, looking up with glazed eyes. "The long trip to Scotland so we could be married—*married*—without publishing banns and all the rest. That ridiculous ceremony, in a stuffy dark parlor with two witnesses off the street. I still wore my ball gown, and it wasn't even clean. The minister used a Bible that was falling apart. What a *joke* it must have seemed to him!"

She rose suddenly, allowing her embroidery hoops

and material and threads to fall on the floor. "And, Aunt Winifred, they were right, in London, weren't they? Lady Jersey and the rest of them were *right*. I was never married."

She left the room hastily, without excusing herself, leaving to her mother and aunt the necessity of explaining her reference about the London gossip to the Duchess.

She climbed the stairs to her room. Tears began before she had flung herself on the bed. Once her head touched the pillow, they came in a flood, wrenching her body, dampening the pillowcase and her handkerchief. Even as she cried, she wondered why she could not stop, why it mattered so much. This morning she had completely forgotten Rodney, the elopement and all the past year's grief. Lawrence loved her, nothing else counted, and the future was glorious. Society's gossip mattered not at all, and whoever had started the *on-dit* would be forced to eat the false words, once she was Lady Harcourt. But now . . .

As the sobs subsided, she sat up, dabbed at her eyes, blew her nose, and tried to think about it rationally. The pain came, surely, from the shattering of the greatest illusion of her life: that her love for Rodney—and his for her—justified the way they had defied convention. Instead, for Rodney, it must have been only a monstrous practical joke.

He had duped her as though she were an adversary he must trick to win a prize (her innocence), and love mattered not at all. And she had been tricked so easily, had capitulated so willingly—yes, he must have laughed. He must have regarded her with a great contempt. She recalled her aunt using that very word in speaking about Rodney—he was "con-

THE UNWELCOME SUITOR 159

temptuous" of Society, perhaps of her. Lawrence, too, had warned her that he was only a man, not a god. Lawrence had . . .

Lawrence had known about the Portuguese wife! He must have known! Perhaps it had been the basis for the quarrel—Rodney boasting of his seduction of her, Lawrence reminding him of an obligation in Portugal. Rodney had disliked obligations, particularly family ones. When she had raised questions about their families' reactions to the elopement, he had said to her, "My parents are both dead. I am responsible only to myself, and that's the way I prefer it." She had commented, half-jokingly, that he wouldn't like being responsible to her, either, but he had retorted, with a roguish, meaningful smile, "You're different, my love." And she had believed him, though she already knew of his impatience with custom, with duties, with obligations of any kind. If Lawrence had reminded him of an obligation to a wife, she could easily imagine his hot-tempered response.

"Why did you quarrel?" she had asked Lawrence. She understood now why he would not tell her. No matter how he might have wished to exonerate himself by putting Rodney in the wrong, he had recognized that in so doing he would have heaped on her the searing sense of shame that was now possessing her. He had refused to do that, preferring to win her on his own merits, sparing her the pain of knowing how monstrously she had been tricked.

She was filled with a great sense of love for Lawrence. And humility. He loved her in spite of her foolishness. She was recognizing, all at once, just how foolish she had been to run away with Rodney. Blind to any signs that might have warned her, blind to anything but the new emotion that had possessed her.

Now it had possessed her again, just this morning. But this time it was, it would be, truly justified. Lawrence was not Rodney. He was going to marry her, and he would never take advantage of her. He had proven that this morning, when the least insistence on his part would have led her to complete surrender.

She thought of his love as an enormous blanket, warming her, shielding her from the world, shielding her from her own ignorance and lack of judgment even as it taught her and made her wise. She longed for the following day, when she would see him again and they could proclaim their love to the world.

15

Thanks to Elena's parting words, it had been necessary for her mother and aunt to explain the debacle of her recent Presentation into London Society to the Duchess of Malvern, whose avid curiosity demanded immediate satisfaction. Lady Theresa finally managed to curtail her friend's shocked lamentations with the excuse that she must see if Elena needed her.

By the time she reached her daughter's bedchamber and knocked on the door, Elena had washed her face clean of tears and powdered her nose and was occupied with brushing her hair. She welcomed her mother into the room with a smile. To Lady Theresa's anxious question as to how she did, she replied that she was quite all right. Then she resumed her seat before her dimity-ruffled dressing table and resumed the attack on her long black tresses.

Not entirely convinced, her mother perched on the damask-covered settee where she could watch Elena's expression in the cheval glass. "If I had known what the Duchess was about to tell you, I wouldn't have . . ." she began.

"It's better that I know," Elena said, giving her

hair a series of particularly vigorous strokes. "I'm *glad* I know."

Lady Theresa nodded approvingly and said, "It *is* for the best, and I'm relieved to see you taking it so calmly. I'm sure it will be a lesson you shan't soon forget—not to throw your cap over the windmill so readily again. A girl needs time to learn about her future husband. A year's engagement is not too long, and she would do well to enlist the judgment of her elders, as well."

Elena didn't answer. She was deciding, quite suddenly, that she ought not give her mother advance warning of Lawrence's proposal, as she had intended. If Lady Theresa were to learn Lord Harcourt had approached her before speaking to her father, she would doubtless accuse him of being as precipitous as Rodney had been. No, this time every detail of her betrothal and marriage must be flawless in the eyes of the world. (Of course, protocol would have barred such impetuous kisses as she had enjoyed this morning, probably until the wedding night itself, but fortunately it was too late to consider that.)

She might have told her father—indeed, she longed to do so more than once—but she never encountered him alone the rest of the day. She did not feel at liberty to interrupt his and the Duke's lengthy discussions of European politics to ask for a private interview, and nothing could have induced her to bring up the subject before his Grace, who would harrumph, look down his long nose at her, call her a sly little baggage, and make his usual stale jokes (always negative) about the married state.

She hugged her happiness to her secretly the rest of the afternoon and evening, suspecting that the only reason it didn't surface of its own buoyancy was

THE UNWELCOME SUITOR 163

because the news of Rodney's perfidy had somehow weighted it, taking some irreplaceable measure of joy from her.

It was more difficult the next morning. Several times at breakfast, with the three older ladies being artificially bright and cheerful for the sake of her supposed state of shock, Elena wanted to laugh at them and say it didn't matter; in an hour or so there would be ample cause for celebration. After they had finished the meal, she secretly took herself down to the kitchen to see if there might be fresh scones or biscuits to serve a midmorning guest. Then she went to her room and took out the unused white vellum-bound diary the Duchess had given her on her last birthday. She would channel her impatience by writing in it the whole history of her acquaintance with Lord Harcourt, surely a worthy beginning if she were ever to use the book.

Sitting at her writing table, she tried to concentrate on organizing her thoughts, but her eyes went all too often to the dainty porcelain clock before her. Her nervousness grew with each passing minute. Ridiculous to be nervous when all she need do was wait for the happy event that was sure to occur.

Eleven o'clock came and went. Perhaps some unexpected problem at Penton Hill had demanded Lawrence's attention. It was disappointing that he must be late for so important an occasion, but she did not doubt he would come.

Noon, and the maid came to her room to announce lunch on the veranda. Elena reluctantly gave up any pretense of diary writing and went to join the others. What a relief that she had said nothing and could keep her anxiety to herself rather than receive the pitying glances of everyone about her. There had been enough of that the day before. And surely he would come in the afternoon. It was merely an unavoidable delay. . . .

But the day waned and fled into night without bringing Lawrence. The next morning Elena rose late, haggard from lack of sleep, and asked the butler if there had been any messages. "None, Miss Elena," Eliot assured her.

If the others noticed her distracted air and lack of appetite at the noon meal, they no doubt thought her still in a pother over the revelation about Rodney. But perhaps they didn't even notice. Lady Theresa, Aunt Winifred, and the Duchess were deep in recollections of their salad days, and the Duke was expounding to her father his theory concerning Napoleon's motives after Waterloo and the British rationale for exiling him to St. Helena rather than America. When Elena asked to be excused from the table, her request was granted absently.

She started for her bedchamber, then changed her mind and wandered into the garden instead. The day was overcast and cooler, which was a relief, but Elena hardly noticed that for the distressing beat of her heart, which had become more pronounced as the slow minutes passed. She realized, with surprise, that she was approaching a state close to panic.

She consulted her pocketwatch. It was one-thirty. Lawrence had said "tomorrow morning." He had also said "without fail." Even had she—or he—mistaken the day, it was long past morning now. His embraces, his words had convinced her of his love, he had asked her to marry him before consulting her father, he had treated their parting as though it were a small death. In short, he had behaved in as passionate a manner as anyone could have wished. Then where was he? News of an accident would have swept the countryside by now. An unexpected duty

THE UNWELCOME SUITOR

or event to prevent his coming would surely have resulted in a letter of explanation, brought to her by one of the army of servants at Penton Hill.

Had she misunderstood? Had she done something unforgiveable? Had he, after sleeping on it, been possessed of second thoughts?

She wandered among the blossoming rose bushes, the tall blue delphiniums, and the yellow coxcombs and tried to remember every moment of their time together two days ago: what she had said, how he had reacted, how he had looked and spoken. She sought meaning from the least gesture or raising of an eyebrow and concluded he had, indeed, behaved like a man in love.

Besides, he had pursued her for over a month, persistent, devoted, patient, wearing down her resistance. Why, when she finally yielded, had he backed away? Had she been deluded again? Rodney had seemed equally persistent, equally in love; yet his actions had been an outrage without parallel. Could Lawrence have lied as Rodney had lied?

Or . . . perhaps he had realized, in spite of his reassuring words, that a man in his position could not, after all, marry a woman who had been deceived into a false marriage and who had herself been involved in deliberately deceiving the *ton*, thereby incurring the censure of the society in which he must move. Perhaps he had concluded that a woman who allowed herself to be part of such a fraud lacked the delicacy of principle necessary to be Viscountess Harcourt. And had she not, possibly, shown herself as too eager, too passionate, not quite the lady after all?

Oh, there were reasons—a veritable mountain of reasons—why he should not, could not, marry her!

Still, her own self-esteem as well as her faith in

Lawrence could not quite believe in any of them. No, something else had happened. There was an explanation, a good one. But she was not sure she could wait for it and remain sane. She hurried into the house on an impulse, thinking to enlist her father's aid. The dining room was deserted, the formal lace cloth and center bowl of pansies and periwinkles all that remained of the setting for the noon meal. Eliot, coming on her in the hall, told her that everyone was having a lie-down, after which the ladies intended to drive into Huntingdon to shop.

Elena knew her father was required to nap every day and she must not interrupt him. She decided quickly, driven by sheer anxiety.

"Eliot, send Jane to me in my room. Then send to the stables and have someone hitch up the tilbury. I mean to drive to Penton Hill in twenty minutes."

She saw a flicker of surprise and disapproval in his eyes, but like the good butler he was, he only said, "Very good, Miss Elena," and went to the servants' quarters. Elena climbed the stairs, trying to decide what costume would befit a bold young woman calling on the man she loved before they were officially engaged.

Elena and Jane set out, not long after the appointed twenty minutes, in the small single-horse open carriage, and arrived at Penton Hill without incident. Her heart in her throat, she watched as Ruggles, who had driven them, repeatedly slammed down the door knocker of the imposing, elaborately carved doors. Except for the clang of brass against brass, everything was quiet; there hardly seemed to be a breeze, and the still damp air seemed to stifle her.

The door opened and she saw Penton Hill's butler

respond to Ruggles' question. The coachman was left waiting on the stoop while the butler consulted someone within; then, after a second exchange between the two servants, Ruggles returned to report to her. "It appears, Miss Elena, that his Lordship is not at home. However, his mother, Mrs. MacLean, will receive you."

His mother! She had not counted on this. The memory of an uncomfortable twenty minutes spent in Mrs. MacLean's London parlor, as well as Lawrence's "The plague take my mother," flashed through her mind. She hesitated, possessed of a distinct impulse to flee.

But no, she must not. This was the woman whose affection she must ultimately win. Besides, who would have better information as to Lawrence's whereabouts?

She turned to Jane, who had been about to descend behind her. "Jane, you may wait here with Ruggles. It appears I shan't be long."

She gained the cool hall of the mansion with no clear idea of what she would say to Mrs. MacLean. It did not lessen her nervousness to suspect that the visit might easily turn into a confrontation.

She was shown a chair in a massive reception room and asked to wait, which she did for a full twenty minutes, becoming anxious and angry by turns, scarcely noticing the magnificence of the room and its appointments. The palms of her hands perspired under her thin white gloves. Finally the doors reopened. Lawrence's mother stopped at the threshold while Elena stood to acknowledge her presence. Her first thought was, Such a little woman to elicit so much anxiety!

"Miss Tyndale! An unexpected pleasure, I'm sure. I thought we had seen the last of you in London." The tone of Mrs. MacLean's voice clearly suggested that she had hoped to have seen the last of Elena in London. Elena forced her body to display a composure she did not feel.

"Good afternoon, Mrs. MacLean. I hope I do not incommode you."

"Not at all. Do be seated." Alice MacLean finally moved into the room—a room that seemed to swallow them up, designed as it had been to easily hold a hundred guests. Lawrence's mother perched on a formal gilded loveseat some distance away, her manner suggesting she could spare her visitor only a few minutes.

"And what may I do for you?" she prompted.

Elena took her seat hesitantly. "I came to—to inquire about Lord Harcourt. He had promised to call yesterday and did not. I—I feared some ill might have befallen him."

Mrs. MacLean smiled. "No ill, so far as I know, Miss Tyndale. But he is not here. Business has taken him to London."

"To London!" Elena echoed, aghast. "Urgent business?"

Mrs. MacLean shrugged; the smile stayed in place. "I really couldn't say. I only arrived Wednesday afternoon; then he was off the next day. Perhaps it had something to do with his servant's death."

Of course! Something urgent had come up because of Justin's death. Still, the explanation didn't ring quite true. If it were only business, surely he would have written her a note to explain his absence.

"Did he say how long he would be gone?"

Again that falsely sympathetic smile, as if in response to the quaver in Elena's voice. "No, I doubt he knew. Possibly several days, possibly longer."

"And he left no message for me?"

"Message for you? Why should he leave a message for you, Miss Tyndale?"

The suddenly unmasked hostility in her tone brought Elena's thoughts to a halt. A smothering silence settled between them.

"Why would he leave you a message?" Mrs. MacLean repeated. "And why had he intended to call? Other than a casual call on neighbors, of course."

"He had asked me to marry him," Elena said in a low voice, "and was to speak to my father."

For a long moment Mrs. MacLean's brown eyes stared unabashedly at Elena, who managed not to look away.

"Oh, I think you must be mistaken, Miss Tyndale," she said at last. "Sadly mistaken, I fear. My son would never do anything so foolish as to marry *you*. You see, I brought him the news from London . . ."

Of course you did, Elena thought. No doubt that was the whole purpose of your trip.

" . . . and I can assure you that, even if he said some trifle to suggest he had serious intentions, they were quickly altered when he learned of your, ah, questionable past."

Elena rose quickly, suddenly more angry than mortified at the woman's insinuations. "The rumors noised about London were falsely slanted, Mrs. MacLean. Lawrence already knew of them and assured me they made no difference in his intentions. And I could not possibly have mistaken a clearly stated proposal of marriage."

Mrs. MacLean, too, stood up. "You forget yourself, young lady. Whatever he said to you, it is quite, *quite* impossible. I would not, under any circumstances, receive a woman with your reputation as my daughter-in-law. And now I must ask you to leave.

I'm afraid your visit has proven extremely disquieting." She turned and left the room without waiting for a response.

Slowly, Elena relaxed the fingers she had unconsciously tightened into fists and took a deep breath. Then she turned and saw a footman in the doorway, waiting to escort her to her carriage. There was nothing to do but leave.

She said nothing during the six-mile trip back to Tyndale Green, except to give Ruggles his instructions. Nor did she look at Jane, who sat beside her with her guileless face well-nigh trembling with unasked questions. When the coachman halted the horse at the side entrance, Elena said, "I am going for a long walk, Jane. Pray advise my mother, if she should ask, that I may not be back in time for tea."

"Shouldna I come wi' ye?" Jane asked anxiously.

"No, indeed, I wish to be by myself. I shan't go far, I assure you." She smiled briefly at Jane, but the maid could not miss the pain in her eyes.

Elena accepted the coachman's hand, descended to the ground, and walked swiftly up the graveled drive to the rear of the house and the garden without a backward look.

16

Mrs. MacLean's arrival at Penton Hill had been as much a surprise to Lawrence as it was to Elena. Returning home from Justin's funeral Wednesday afternoon, his thoughts had been centered on gaining the cool house after sweltering under a relentless sun in black arm-banded frock coat at the gravesite. He sorely needed rest, for he hadn't snatched more than a couple of dozes the past thirty-six hours. Above all, he wished time to savor the amazing good fortune the morning's encounter with Elena had brought him. How ironic that his energies must be taken up all day with funeral arrangements and mourning when joy filled him to bursting. But then, fate was a master at spilling out elation and misery in great, untidy mixtures, careless of the appropriateness of the occasion.

And so he arrived at Penton Hill's west entrance and was greeted by Wiggins, his butler, who opened the door for him, bowed, and said, "My Lord, Mrs. MacLean and the Lady Cordelia have arrived."

"Great God," Lawrence muttered to himself in dismay. Then, more directly to the servant, "How long ago? I hope their wants have been attended to."

"Yes, my Lord, they have been taken to the two

171

adjoining bedchambers in the north wing and given refreshments. Mrs. Roberts was in a taking because you had failed to notify her of their coming."

"That's because I didn't know of it myself, Wiggins. Where are they now?"

"Her Ladyship is resting. Mrs. MacLean is awaiting you on the veranda. She spoke of a matter of some urgency . . ."

"I'll be there directly . . . No, I must bathe and change first. It's hot as Hades today in the sun. Tell her I'll join her in half an hour. Thank you, Wiggins."

He took the stairs to his own chambers slowly, reluctant to shave any time off that half-hour. A matter of some urgency. What could it be this time that would bring his mother and Cordelia over the long dusty road from London on a hot summer's day rather than sending a servant with a message?

By the time he came to her on the veranda Lawrence had come to the hopeful conclusion that the urgency was in her own mind and whatever he would be called upon to do could wait awhile, at least until after he had spoken to Sir John Tyndale and secured his pledge that he and Elena might marry. And then he remembered Elena's anticipation of his mother's objections to the match. "We must have her blessing, too." He sighed. He might as well face it now, for delay would only make the matter more difficult.

At the sound of his footsteps on the black-and-white tile, Mrs. MacLean turned from contemplating the sculptured gardens and statuary beyond the veranda to greet her son. "Ah, Lawrence, at last! I was grieved to hear about Justin. How does his widow?"

"As well as can be expected right now, Mother. How was your trip?" He bent and kissed her cheek.

THE UNWELCOME SUITOR 173

"Quite, quite awful. The heat, you know. Cordelia is prostrate. I hope she will recover in time for supper. You know how she dislikes travel."

"Then why did she—why did you come? What has happened? You knew I would be returning to London in a day or two."

Mrs. MacLean sighed and shook her head, shading her eyes with a gesture calculated to arouse his pity. "I suppose it was foolish of me, and, oh, Lawrence, I do apologize for bursting in on you like this but . . . it's Lambert."

"Lambert? There's been some kind of accident?" Lawrence's voice took on a real alarm. His affection for his younger brother had always been strong in spite of the twelve years' difference in their ages.

"No, nothing like that, except the accident of his incurable mischievousness. Truly, Lawrence, that child is the bane of my existence. Pray sit down a minute. Read this." She searched in her reticule and brought out a letter, which she handed to him.

Frowning, Lawrence took it and sat opposite her in a chair. The letter, from Eton's provost, was curt and to the point.

Dear Madam,
   It is my painful duty to inform you that your son, Lambert Edward MacLean, is hereby dismissed from Eton College for mutinous conduct directed against the headmaster on June 8. The seriousness of his misbehavior precludes his return to this school, showing, as it does, that Master Lambert is unhappily possessed of a violent and malicious nature, and that he has no respect for those in authority. Details of his crime, as well as the deliberations of myself and

the other masters concerning it, will be forthcoming in a separate letter.

I have directed Master Lambert to remain in his rooms until he is fetched home. We will appreciate your earliest cooperation in the matter of his departure.

I remain, Madame,
Your obed't. etc. etc.

"Expelled!" Lawrence shook his head in disbelief. "Is that possible? What could he have done? Most of the boys are mischievous. I know I was when I attended. One is expected to get into scrapes."

"I haven't an inkling," Mrs. MacLean said shortly. "All I know is that boy was trying deliberately to humiliate me. He has always . . ."

"Oh, Mother, that's coming it a trifle strong!"

"Deliberately, Lawrence."

"Have you contacted him, then? Sent a servant?"

"I sent Murphy for him yesterday, before we left. No doubt they are on their way now. I said we would meet him here, at Penton Hill."

"Here? But, Mother . . ."

"Just temporarily. You must help me in this, Lawrence. He won't heed me, his own mother, anymore. He threatens to run away to the Navy and I don't know what foolishness else, if I so much as frown at him. But he still admires you, Lawrence. You are his *beau idéal.*" She stopped to dab at her eyes with a handkerchief.

Lawrence threw her a veiled glance, nonplussed at the way he had suddenly turned into chief guardian and mentor for his brother. Not so long ago he had been the unruly one, the one who had escaped his mother's watchful eye by himself running away to the Army.

"Yes, I understand," he said finally. "What would you have me do, then?"

"Just talk to him. Persuade him he must settle down and forgo these wretched mischiefs. I suppose we shall need a private tutor now—a strict one. I want you to help me find one. I doubt any school will take him again, with his record for getting into scrapes, and he will never settle down and study for university without a master to beat it into him."

"Has it ever occurred to you, Mother, that Lambert may not want to go to university?"

"Oh, stuff and nonsense, he must. All gentlemen must have an education, especially if they are not to inherit a title or money—and you know your father left precious little money. I have always thought he would do very well at the law, if need be, but if he don't wish that, he must at least have a good classical education and make the right contacts. I'll take him home to Crafton Hall and make sure he toes the mark. The school may have given up on him, but I shan't. There will be no outings, no sweets, no holidays, until he has proven himself."

Lawrence could not hide a frown. "Mother, I venture to suggest you are a bit harsh. I promise to speak to him, but at least wait until we hear his side of it before you sentence him."

"I did expect your cooperation in this."

"I am cooperating. I only ask a little forbearance from you. And while we are on the subject of forbearance, I must ask your indulgence on *my* behalf . . ."

He forced a smile in her direction, but she was too full of her own concern to recognize his change of topic. She went on, "As for bringing Cordelia with me, we had decided to return to Crafton Hall anyway —this only precipitated the move. She was not enjoying London, especially when you weren't there to..."

"You're both welcome," he broke in, afraid of what she might say next. "But do listen, Mother, to what I have to say." He moved uneasily to the edge of his chair.

She frowned at his interruption but leaned back and gave him her full attention at last. "What is it, dear?"

He plunged in without any preliminaries. "I have asked Miss Tyndale to marry me, and she has honored me by agreeing. I am going to see her father tomorrow morning, to ask his permission."

He realized as he spoke that he had taken her completely unawares. She stared at him for several long moments in utter shock. Her mouth opened and closed twice before a sound came out of it. When it did, the sound was predictable. "Lawrence, how *could* you?"

"I love her. It's as basic as that. She is beautiful and intelligent and utterly charming, but what has that to do with it? I simply know she will suit me absolutely."

"You know nothing of the kind! You've scarcely met her. And you are totally ignoring the . . . Of course! You left London before the rumor spread. Still, I warned you, did I not?"

"Warned me of what?" he asked innocently.

"Of her reputation, her past. But now it is even worse. The news is all over London. You would be laughed out of every drawing room in . . ."

"Shall I? Mother, who started the rumor?"

"I have no idea." But her eyes were evasive. "What does it matter? You cannot afford to ignore . . ."

"But I do." He stood as he spoke, decisively. "I do ignore it, and I shall."

She rose also, not quite reaching to his shoulder

THE UNWELCOME SUITOR

but undaunted by such a disadvantage. "You have not thought this through, Lawrence. You are allowing your emotions to take possession of your senses. Now listen, for a change, before you make a mull of your life. Only consider what Miss Tyndale has done. She eloped with some officer and lived with him in sin until he abandoned her. She has taken part in an unforgivable deception, suppressing her past, being presented to the best Society. And you would conveniently restore her reputation by *marrying* her! No wonder she is overjoyed at your proposal."

"Mother, you do *not* know . . ."

"She is lovely, I admit," Mrs. MacLean conceded, paying no attention to his interruption. "But that is just the trouble. She is far too lovely for men to ignore. Once married to you, it is inevitable that she would be propositioned from time to time, especially as her past indiscretions are so well known. And believe me, Lawrence, a woman who has deceived before will deceive again! Who knows but what she will turn to some jaded roué with a handsome face, once the glamour of being married to you has worn off? Can you really ignore the possibility of being monstrously *deceived?* Think about *that* for a while!"

But her warnings of dire consequences only aroused Lawrence's impatience. "Mother, this is too much! You have swallowed a number of incredible tales about Miss Tyndale without the slightest proof. Now, I truly regret I cannot do as you wish and marry Cordelia. I apologize for that, if I must. But I must remind you that I would not marry her in any case. Even if I never marry Miss Tyndale, I shall assuredly not marry Lady Cordelia. Are you equally ready to oppose any woman in the land who is not the Lady Cordelia Radcliffe?"

"Lawrence, I have only wished to warn you . . ."

"And you have, indeed, warned me. Now do me the kindness of allowing yourself to at least *conceive* of Miss Tyndale as your daughter-in-law, without consideration of these preposterous rumors. And after you have done so, we shall talk of it further. It is agreed?" He smiled at her engagingly, although, at the moment, he was more inclined to shake her.

She drew in an injured sniff. "I shall certainly agree to talk of it again, and hope to bring you to your senses. I hope you realize how unhappy you have made me. On top of this business with Lambert . . ."

He leaned over and kissed her upturned face gently. "My dear Mother, you will be happy enough in time, I assure you. Meanwhile, I must speak to Wiggins about arrangements for Lambert, since he may arrive here shortly. I trust you will make yourself at home, and I'll see you at supper."

17

They had just been seated for supper—which was late, awaiting Lady Cordelia's tardy recovery from her journey—when a footman, claiming an emergency, interrupted them to admit Mrs. MacLean's servant, Murphy. He stopped at the doorway, red-faced and cap in hand, his clothes travel-stained, and addressed Mrs. MacLean in distressed tones, his eyes on the floor.

"Bad news, mum. The young master's missin'. He wasna at t'boardin'house when I went to fetch 'im, nor anywhere about t'school or village. 'Is roommate says 'e run away i' the night."

"Run away!" The echoing words seemed torn from Mrs. MacLean's throat. Lawrence glanced in dismay from the servant to his mother in time to see her start up in alarm, her hand at her throat, then fall back into her chair in a dead faint.

It seemed to Lawrence an interminable length of time before she came around. The two footmen hastened to help him carry her inert form to a sofa in the small family parlor adjoining the dining room. Lady Cordelia hastened after them and knelt anxiously by her side, wafting her own vinaigrette, which she always carried with her, under Mrs.

MacLean's nose. Lawrence chaffed his mother's wrists and massaged her forehead and called for the housekeeper. Still she remained white and quite unconscious until Mrs. Roberts arrived and laid cold cloths on her temples. Then she stirred and moaned and suddenly raised a hand to grasp Lawrence's arm.

"Find him," she whispered with startling presence of mind. "You must find him!"

"Of course we'll find him, Mother. Surely he'll turn up . . ."

"You must go yourself, at once. It can't be left to the servants. Oh, I shall die if the poor child is hurt or . . . worse. There are footpads and highwaymen. Where could he have gone? Where? Do you think he meant that, about the Navy? Where does one *go* to join the Navy, anyway?"

Flailing her arms, she insisted on sitting up, forcing Lawrence to move back. She ignored Lady Cordelia's gentle protest that she remain quiet, and grasped Lawrence's hand. "Promise me you'll go," she repeated urgently. "It can't be left to the servants. Promise me."

"Yes, yes, Mother, I'll go," he reassured her. "Pray don't distress yourself. I'll start immediately. Surely there will be a clue at Eton as to where he went. Perhaps he has been found by now."

"Let us pray heaven you are right, Lawrence," she returned. "But you must go quickly and bring him back. I shan't have a moment's peace until I see him again." She dropped her head into her hands and began sobbing. "Oh, Lambert, my baby, why did you do this? What has happened to you?"

Lady Cordelia put an arm about her hunched shoulders in an attempt at comfort. Then she looked up at Lawrence. He thought he saw in her eyes a glimmer of suspicion, echoing his own, that his mother's show of emotion was excessive, but then her eyebrows shot up as though asking him why he stood there like a dolt when he should already be on his way.

He bent quickly to kiss the top of his mother's head, then turned and called for Wiggins, who waited just outside in the hall. Starlight must be saddled at once; cook must pack some food for him to eat on the way; his valet must help him out of his dinner clothes and into riding leathers. Then he called to Murphy to accompany him to his room and fill him in on particulars as he dressed. Action was easy, far easier than dealing with women's fears. He was glad to be a man, to be able to act. It helped relieve some of his own anxiety.

Lawrence arrived on the northern outskirts of London about the same time as did the farmers' fruit and vegetable carts and the cattle and sheep destined for the butchers' knives. He had spent the remainder of the evening and a good portion of the night on one post horse after another, catching only two hours' rest at an inn in Biggleswade. Most of the time he had been benumbed with anxiety or sheer weariness. Now, as he was forced to slow his pace because of the traffic, he tried to sort out what action he must take in the next few hours. And he kept returning to the nagging conviction that he had failed to do something important before leaving Penton Hill. He'd gone over it again and again, but his mind seemed in a fog and he could think of nothing more to do for Lambert than race to find him.

Suddenly it came to him: he had promised Elena that this very morning he would call on Sir John Tyndale to ask for her hand in marriage. "Without fail," he had vowed. He swore in self-disgust as he urged the horse through the press in the City. It seemed unbelievable that anything could have driven thoughts of Elena from his mind, but now he saw how it had happened. His mother's well-calculated hysteria over Lambert's disappearance had driven him off in a mad rush to London before he could collect his wits, which had been scattered enough from lack of sleep. He had not even done the obvious—sent her a message explaining the necessity of his absence.

Now here he was, groggy with fatigue, disheveled with travel, surrounded by produce wagons lumbering toward Covent Gardens, delayed by the incoming of great scarlet mail coaches overladen with luggage and riders, halted by importunate beggars or vendors of pigeon pies and gingerbread whenever he slowed his pace—and quite helpless to rectify the terrible omission.

His sense of urgency concerning Lambert had already begun to dwindle, replaced by the suspicion that the young rascal knew well enough what he was about, and had no intention of running away to the Navy, where discipline was considerably more onerous than at school. Instead, he may well have been hiding out somewhere simply to give his mother a good scare.

Leaving his post horse at Mr. Tilbury's livery stable, he took a hackney cab to the Clairmont, where he planned to enlist his man, Claxton, to search likely places in London for the boy. One of Claxton's hearty breakfasts would, he hoped, restore him enough to continue to Eton astride a fresh horse from his own stables, where he would interview whomever he could find for clues to Lambert's whereabouts.

Rain had threatened since dawn and he felt the first sprinkles as he turned off Oxford Street into Mayfair. Foul weather was all he needed to delay him further, he thought angrily. What a miserable twenty-four hours it had been, bringing him down all too swiftly from the Olympian heights to which he and Elena had soared only a brief morning past. The memory of her kisses redoubled his impatience with his brother, his mother, and the chain of circumstances that had forced him to remain separated from her. And what would be her reaction when he didn't appear as he had promised?

By the time he arrived at Clarges Street the rain was steady and hard. The horse drawing the cab stumbled on the slick, wet paving stones as they turned a corner, and Lawrence's boots splattered into a puddle as he hurriedly descended and paid the driver. He dashed into the building, dreading the next leg of his journey in such a downpour.

Claxton answered his ring with an uncharacteristic exclamation of relief. "My Lord! You have arrived at last!"

"I have, indeed," Lawrence agreed, remembering he had first expected to return to London two days ago. He allowed the servant to pull off his damp riding coat. "I shan't be staying long, I'm afraid. Be so good as to start some eggs and tea, and I'll fill you in while I eat."

"Very good, my Lord, but first I must warn you that you have a visitor."

"A visitor?" Lawrence glanced quickly about the sitting room, but it held only the two of them.

"Not here, my Lord. I took the liberty of allowing him to use your bed. He was that bone weary, he never waited for a bite to eat before he was off . . ."

His voice died away as Lawrence, hope invading his gloom, strode down the short hall to his bedchamber, opened the door, and looked over at the bed.

Lambert was sleeping soundly under the counterpane, his face flushed and slightly grimy, his fair hair tousled about his ears and forehead as though it had not had a combing in two days.

"When did he arrive?" he asked in a low tone of wonder.

Claxton, who had followed him discreetly, answered from the doorway, "Just this morning, my Lord, about dawn. His clothes were that muddy and torn, I took him for a footpad. But he'd a letter from you convinced me he was your brother."

Immeasurable relief swept Lawrence, and with it new consciousness of a dizzying headache, an immense weariness, and a stomach that clamored for food. He retreated out the door, closing it softly behind him. "Thank God," he said. It was the most heartfelt prayer he had uttered in some time. "Well, Claxton, it looks as though you must make me up a bed on the sofa—or your own bed, if I may—for I need a sleep myself. But first, the food."

Unlike Lambert, he managed to stay awake long enough to devour three fried eggs, most of a kidney pie, and two pears, washed down with tea. Then, half-undressed, he fell into his servant's bed and slept, with a singlemindedness not unlike his Army days, until suppertime.

"All right, young man, I want the whole story," Lawrence told his brother as they finished a late supper. They were seated opposite each other at the small table in his sitting room, where they had just shared a chicken and some of Gunther's famous pastries. Lawrence's tone was severe. In spite of the truce while they ate, Lambert could tell his brother meant business, and he dare not delay the confrontation further.

"Will you believe me?"

"Of course I'll believe you," Lawrence said, surprised Lambert would think otherwise. "But I want facts, not fustian. All I know now is that you behaved in a mutinous manner to Dr. Keate and the provost has concluded you have a 'violent and malicious nature.' He also, if I recall rightly, called your behavior a crime, but did not specify. Just what did you do to the poor headmaster?"

"I hit him."

"You hit him?" Lawrence repeated, incredulously. "You *hit* him? Attacked him *physically?*"

"Now, Lawrence, there's no need to come the ugly. Yes, I hit him, with his own birch rod. I daresay it was rum of me, but I couldn't *stand* it." His jaw, which was like his mother's, protruded defiantly. "You see, he was flogging Washburn, and Washburn was innocent. I'd told Dr. Keate so, and he wouldn't believe me. Said it wouldn't hurt the lad, he'd probably something else to be guilty about. The thing is, Lawrence, he wouldn't take my word for it against the word of Chambers, who's a gabble-monger. But I knew Washburn hadn't done it because he was with me . . ."

"Done what?"

"Put toads in Mr. Evers' bed—he's our tutor."

"Oh." Lawrence tried not to smile.

"Mr. Evers is gooseish about toads."

"And someone was trying to help him get over it?"

"It was probably Chambers himself. It wasn't me, I swear it," Lambert said. "But I couldn't stand seeing Washburn getting flogged for something he didn't do. You see, it was my turn as praeposter, and another boy and I had to hold him down for the flogging because he was trying to wriggle out of it. I couldn't stand it, so I grabbed the cane away and . . . I only hit the headmaster once, not apurpose, but then he started after me and I just . . . I—I'd much rather not go back, Lawrence. Dr. Keate does seem to enjoy the flogging so."

"I rather think you've no choice, old boy. They won't take you back after this roguery. It showed shocking lack of respect, whatever your excuse."

"I know." But there was a tinge of self-satisfaction in Lambert's voice. He had grown very tall in his fifteenth year. Being a member of the rowing club as well as an avid player of cricket and fives had, no doubt, developed his muscles marvelously. Lawrence had no trouble believing he had been fully capable of overpowering an irascable headmaster whose reputation for indiscriminate caning was notorious. But he was surprised that Lambert seemed quite unabashed by what he had done.

"Aren't you even ashamed?" Lawrence asked.

Lambert looked back at him sullenly. "I apologized. He made me. I got twice as many lashes with that birch as Washburn got, so you needn't think I didn't pay. But I'm *not* sorry, and I'd never go back there, even if they were to let me. Although it's a shame, in a way. I was sure to get Captain of the Boats next term if I'd stayed."

"An apology is hardly enough for such an act," Lawrence said thoughtfully, fingering his empty wineglass. "*Mater* is sure to fly up in the boughs over this, once she recovers from the fright you've given her."

"Oh, I daren't tell her," Lambert cried out. "You won't cry rope on me, will you? That's why I ran away."

"And just where did you think you were going?"

"Well, first I thought to go to the coast and join the Navy."

THE UNWELCOME SUITOR

"A bird-witted choice, but never mind."

"So I scoured off toward Portsmouth. It was easy at first. I jumped on behind a cabbage wagon, and the driver never knew. But then I collected he wasn't going south any longer, so I jumped off and began walking. Only I got turned around and found myself back near the Thames. And then I met a limey and told him what I wanted to do. And he warned me off it. He said they flog you even worse in the Navy if you get caught up."

"I should think so."

"So I rather dropped the idea. And I was getting devilish hungry, and I'd lost my purse, so I decided to come see you. Especially after it started to rain and I hadn't any place to stay." His lips trembled and Lawrence recognized that his brief experience as a homeless wanderer had possibly held some terrors that he was not yet ready to recount.

"We will have to tell Mother, nevertheless," Lawrence said. "And you must take your medicine like a man. It won't be so bad as a flogging, I promise you."

"Sometimes, with Mama, it's worse. She never lets one *forget*."

Lawrence laughed; the boy had put it so right.

Seizing on his apparent good humor, Lambert said, "I say, Lawrence, can't you hire me a tutor so I'll pass my exams for King's College . . ."

"I rather expect that's what Mother intends for you."

"I mean, let me live at Penton Hill instead of going back to Crafton Hall with Mama? I'd be a proper brick, Lawrence, really. I'll study so hard you won't know me."

"It would be a change," Lawrence acknowledged dryly. "We'll see what Mama says."

"Oh, the deuce take . . ."

"Lambert," Lawrence interrupted before he could finish the blasphemy. The boy looked up, startled. "I'm on your side," Lawrence assured him.

Some time later, when Lawrence, in unconscious penance for his sternness, had settled into a game of chess with Lambert, the door knocker sounded. He looked up as Claxton answered it and was surprised to see Stuart Jaeger in the doorway.

"Ask him in, Claxton," he said, rising.

"I saw your light," Jaeger explained, handing Claxton his dripping umbrella. "And thought I'd stop by before retiring and let you know . . ."

He stopped as his eyes went to Lambert. Lawrence introduced them and sent the boy to the bedchamber, suggesting he get more sleep so they could start the trip back to Penton Hill at dawn. Then he turned back to Jaeger. "Come in, come in, have a drink." He waved his guest to a chair and went to the cellarette for a bottle of porter.

In spite of his cordial invitation, Lawrence was not particularly happy to see Stuart Jaeger just now. The man's appearance reminded him all too vividly of his broken promise to Elena. He had not written an explanation from London, realizing he would be home as soon as any letter he might post to her, but in spite of that, he chaffed at the delay in returning. By himself he might even have risked another night ride and all that entailed of discomfort and muddy roads in the rain, which had not slackened all day, simply to be with her more quickly. But with Lambert, a poor horseman, such a daredevil ride would be foolhardy, and he had no intention of leaving the boy behind to think up further harebrained schemes to escape his mother's justice.

So they would have to go post-chaise and hope the

roads would prove passable after all the rain. If all went well—if the sun came out and the carriage didn't lose a wheel or run into an unexpected quagmire—he could hope to see Elena again by teatime, explain his prolonged absence, and perhaps hold her in his arms. The prospect filled him with an immense longing.

If all went well. He was not sure why his thoughts dwelt on that reservation with a kind of dread that hovered about him during most of Jaeger's visit.

"I received your message about being delayed at Penton Hill," Jaeger explained. "And thought you might like to know that the little expedition to Astley's Circus last Tuesday didn't get completely scotched."

"It didn't?" Lawrence was startled by the reference. The equestrian show seemed a millennium in the past.

Jaeger was grinning in more than friendliness now. "I managed to persuade Miss Saxton to go, anyway. Or, rather, I made the proposal to her father, who had expressed interest in the Hungarian riders himself. He decided, contrary to Lady Saxton's wishes, that his daughter should have the privilege of seeing them, too. So the three of us went."

"I'm not sure a girl's father would be my favorite chaperon," Lawrence commented, sipping his drink.

"On the contrary, it was capital! We talked horses all evening, when we weren't watching them. It was a truly amazing exhibition. And Miss Saxton is quite the dab, not only about horses but about all sorts of country affairs. She is remarkable. I'm beginning to believe that she would do for me much better than any delicately bred city lass, since I shall probably spend most of my life in the country. And her father and I got on splendidly, so there should be no problem in that direction."

"You have the whole matter wrapped up already?"

"Hardly!" Jaeger laughed. "But I've a feeling it's just around the corner. One can sense these things."

"Can one!" Lawrence marveled and took another swallow of porter. "Well, I'd go bail Miss Tyndale will be pleased."

"Miss Tyndale!" Jaeger looked a little put off.

"Yes. It was her idea, actually, that you and Miss Saxton would be well-suited to each other."

"The devil you say! But then, do you know the *on-dit* about Miss Tyndale?"

"What are they saying?" Lawrence asked, his voice suddenly tense.

"That she'd had a love-child with some fellow or other that she eloped with. And that, of course, means not only is she no lady, but Lord love us, she committed the cardinal sin of gaining admittance to the *ton* under false pretenses."

Jaeger's undertone of sarcasm only underscored his studied nonchalance, as if he were talking of none better than a barmaid who had gotten herself in the family way. Lawrence had difficulty controlling his rising anger.

"Where did the rumor start?" he asked brusquely.

"Ah, Lady Jersey, I believe."

"And where did she hear it?" Lawrence shot at him.

Jaeger's eyebrows lifted at his tone. "No need to get into a pelter, Harcourt. *I'm* not the bloody gabble-monger, and I've no idea who is. Miss Saxton heard it from Lady Jersey. Didn't believe a word of it herself, you understand."

"Do you believe it?"

THE UNWELCOME SUITOR

"I shouldn't think it matters to me one way or another," Jaeger returned in a placating voice. "But I did think the story had rather a nasty ring to it. Sorry if I offended." His eyes were on Lawrence speculatively over the rim of the glass.

"Miss Tyndale and I are engaged to wed," Lawrence said curtly, leaping to his feet. "Kindly apologize for what you just said or leave this room."

"See here, Harcourt, I hope you don't imagine . . . I was only repeating . . . You asked me . . ."

"The story is false in any event." As Jaeger continued to stare at him in dismayed astonishment, Lawrence's eyes lost their angry flame. He leaned over and took his visitor's empty glass. "You must excuse me, I know you're not to blame. I already knew the *on-dit* from Miss Tyndale herself, but it sounds even more beastly from someone else's lips. By the bye, in case you doubted her, let me assure you she is very much a lady, and I consider myself the luckiest man in the world." He refilled Jaeger's glass and held it out to him, daring him to challenge the statement.

Jaeger hesitated only a moment, then jumped to his feet to accept the glass. "Forgive me, old chap. Heartiest congratulations! To make amends, may I . . . may I propose a toast? To Miss Tyndale."

Lawrence refilled his own goblet, managed a smile, and lofted it toward the other's. "And to Miss Saxton. Two charming ladies."

"May we both be noosed within a year!"

"If not sooner," Lawrence agreed.

18

Lawrence and Lambert, riding post-chaise, arrived at Penton Hill just past four in the afternoon. The sky had remained cloud-filled but rainless. Mrs. MacLean fussed over both of them with great tears of joy in her eyes. Then, her demeanor grown stern, she signaled her youngest to accompany her into the library for a full accounting of all that had transpired. Lambert, his homecoming exuberance squashed, threw a mute appeal to Lawrence.

"No use trying to fob off now," Lawrence told him cheerfully. "Just bear up. And remember, the truth, without any humbug."

Lambert nodded glumly and followed his mother into the library. Lawrence turned away to find Lady Cordelia coming toward him. In her usual self-effacing way she had not interfered with the reunion between mother and sons other than to speak a few quiet words of welcome to both of them.

"And are you quite recovered from your journey?" he remembered to ask her.

She smiled shyly. "Quite recovered. How could I not be? You have been to London and back while I simply rusticated here. Penton Hill is so delightful, and it's no end of a relief to be away from London and the constant social demands."

"Don't you care for it at all, then—the routs and such?"

"Not at all. I am a queer goose, I suppose. There are a number of things everyone else seems to consider essential that I am quite certain I don't like, or shouldn't like, but I find it difficult to convince Cousin Alice of my feelings."

"Such as?" he asked.

She shook her head. "Oh . . . things," she said vaguely. He thought a slight blush came to her cheek.

"Will you excuse me? I have a rather pressing errand. I must be off at once to Tyndale Green."

"Oh?" She looked startled. "But you only just arrived."

"Yes, but . . . Didn't Mother tell you?" Seeing her eyes vacant of understanding, he hurried on, "I have asked Miss Tyndale to marry me, and . . ." He broke off, remembering his mother's certainty that Lady Cordelia doted on him. Had he just been unbelievably callous?

But she did not appear stunned or hurt, only pleased. "Indeed! Then I must offer my congratulations." She held out a cousinly hand, which he grasped gratefully.

"She didn't mention it to you?"

"Not at all," she said.

"Then she still expects I'll change my mind. But I shan't. You . . . you aren't overset or likely to wear the willow, are you?" He looked at her anxiously. "She gave me a good scold for not asking you. She led me to believe . . ."

Cordelia was shaking her head and smiling. "I *do* love you, Lawrence, but not in that way." It was the most spontaneous thing he had ever heard her say. She was postively beaming and had become, in an instant, quite animated and pretty. "It is such a relief because, owing so much to your mother as I do, I didn't want to be the one to spoil her hopes. I would have had trouble refusing you if you had asked me, so this is much better." Her voice started to peter out, as though she had just realized how bold she had been to discuss such a topic with him.

"Then someone else has spoken for you?" Lawrence suggested hopefully.

"No, no one else. I simply do not wish to marry at all."

He thought it an odd thing for a girl to say. "You're quite sure?"

"Absolutely sure. I've been sure for a long while, but I never . . . It's one of the things I'm a queer goose about, I suppose. But I've never seen the need for it. I'm quite content living with Cousin Alice. She's all the family I wish for. I have plenty of money, and this way I needn't . . . needn't . . ."

She got stuck again and looked away from him, embarrassed. Lawrence guessed, suddenly, that the intimacy of the marriage bed might be the inhibiting factor, and decided the topic was best left at that. He wanted to hug her for her unexpected confession, but perhaps that would have been unwelcome as too forward a response. He contented himself with a quick, chaste kiss on her forehead before she retreated back into her shell.

"Then perhaps together we can convince Mother I've not broken your heart."

"Of course. I'll do what I can."

"Now I really must be off. You see, I had promised Miss Tyndale I'd address her father yesterday morning. She may have given up expecting me by now."

"Oh! Then that explains why . . ." Lady Cordelia put her hand to her mouth in a sudden, stricken gesture.

"What?" Lawrence asked sharply while premonitory chills shot through his spine.

"Miss Tyndale called this afternoon. I didn't see her, but I saw her leave from my upstairs sitting room."

"She *called*?"

"Yes. Cousin Alice saw her. And I . . . I don't know what was said between them, but I saw Miss Tyndale's face in profile as she got into her carriage and she looked quite distressed. And then I encountered your mother in the hall, and she said—forgive me, Lawrence, I didn't connect it all until now. She told me to congratulate her, for she believed she had just prevented you from making the gravest error of your life."

Lawrence burst into the library without bothering to knock. Lambert, his gangling height towering over his seated mother, relaxed his shamefaced stance and threw him a glad startled glance. Mrs. MacLean frowned.

"Lawrence, for shame!" was all she could utter before he strode across the room to her chair and stopped before her with a frightening abruptness, livid anger in his face. She had the sensation that, had he not stopped himself, he might have leaned over, grabbed her shoulders, and cruelly shaken her.

"Mother, how could you!"

"How could I what, dear? And where are your manners? Can't you see . . ."

Lawrence turned to Lambert. "Go along to your room. I'm sure this can wait. We have somewhat more urgent business."

Lambert scooted out of the room readily enough while Mrs. MacLean said indignantly, "Lawrence, have you lost your wits? How dare you barge in while I'm disciplining my son."

"It can wait," Lawrence repeated harshly. "I want to know just what you said to Miss Tyndale when she called this afternoon."

Mrs. MacLean glanced to the door a second time and saw Lady Cordelia hovering just outside it. "Cordelia told you . . ."

"Yes, Cordelia told me Miss Tyndale was here. What did you tell her? Did you explain my absence?"

Mrs. MacLean was about to chastise her son for the overly loud way he was addressing her, but something in his eyes stopped her. Instead, she tried to pacify him. "I simply told her the truth. That you went to London on business."

"Did you tell her what that business was? Why it was so urgent?"

"I did not. It was none of her affair."

He took a deep breath, thereby avoiding the profanity that came to his lips, and prayed for patience. "But I had told you of my intentions to speak to her father. Surely you knew she came here out of a great concern when I never appeared. Good God! Now she doubtless thinks I simply went off on a whim, forgetting my promise to her, and with no explanation. She must think me the most heartless wretch!"

"Let her! I'm sorry, Lawrence, but it's all to the good if she thinks ill of you. You see, I am quite resolved not to see you make a fool of yourself, especially when you could make me—and everyone —so happy by marrying your dear cousin."

"May not that dear cousin have something to say in the matter?"

THE UNWELCOME SUITOR

Lawrence heard the hesitant voice behind him in amazement and half-turned as Lady Cordelia came to stand beside him, her hands clasped tightly before her. She turned her large, scared eyes toward him as though for courage. He gave her a grateful smile. His mother seemed too surprised for words.

Lady Cordelia returned her gaze to the woman seated before them. "C-cousin Alice, I love you dearly and—and would do anything rather than cross you," she began hesitantly. "But—but I have never wished to marry your son and I must tell you now"—her voice grew the least bit bolder—"I *cannot* marry him."

Cousin Alice favored her with a cold glance, at which Lady Cordelia seemed to wilt. "Indeed? Why not, pray? Do you find him repulsive?"

"Oh, no, indeed! It's just that I don't—don't wish to marry *anyone*." The end of her sentence had grown faint, yet she managed to emphasize the last word.

Mrs. MacLean glanced suspiciously from her to Lawrence. "You are both hoaxing me."

"No hoax," Lawrence took up. "We only wish to make you see that you cannot order other peoples' lives for them. We are telling you the truth, and you must accept it. Cordelia and I are friends and cousins, only that. It's all we'll ever be to each other."

"My dear Cordelia, do you swear this is true? He hasn't set you up for it?"

Lady Cordelia managed to shake her head vigorously and then, in case Cousin Alice had mistaken which question she was answering, added faintly, "He speaks truly, Cousin."

Slowly Mrs. MacLean returned her gaze to her son, her bosom heaving with agitation. Finally she gave a great sigh. "Oh, very well, my dears! I cannot fight the both of you. But as for accepting Miss Tyndale, that is imposs—"

"Your arguments against Miss Tyndale don't pass current, Mother," Lawrence interrupted. "I know the truth about her past much better than do you." His voice grew measured and emphatic. "I must insist again—the rumors are false. It is true she eloped with Captain Farnsworth, but she married him in good faith. Her retirement to the country soon after was to mourn his death . . ."

Here, Lawrence's voice faltered the least bit. He had never given his mother any hint concerning his part in the captain's death, even successfully concealing that he had been the object of a magisterial investigation. But now she only stared at him with a cold surprise that seemed to spring more from his daring to argue with her than from what he was saying.

"Miss Tyndale was nearly destroyed by his terrible fate, an unforeseeable accident," he continued. "She came to London for the Season with the utmost reluctance, only because her family urged her to it. As for myself, I have—with God's help, I suspect—finally persuaded her she need not mourn him forever. She has, at last, given me a chance to make her happy. I have fought a battle with a dead man for her, Mother, and I will not be thwarted now. You simply must accept her, for both our sakes. And for Cordelia's sake as well."

She was amazed by the passion of his words. "Well, really, Lawrence, I . . ."

"And I wish you to come with me right now," Lawrence hurried on, "so that you may apologize for your attitude toward her. She has said she cannot marry me without your blessing. You will have to

THE UNWELCOME SUITOR 199

convince her you give it genuinely, that you retract your unkind words . . ."

"That is going too far!"

"No, it is not." His glance grew fierce. He leaned over her abruptly and gripped both her shoulders, but stopped short of shaking them. "You have much to apologize for. I think I know now where that rumor came from, Mother. I shall not press you on it, nor demand a confession, but you *will* come with me. Now." He stood back and waited, a rock that would not be moved.

She made one or two more excuses, but they were puny things, a last resistance to salvage her self-respect. It was the realization that he knew she was the source of the gossip about Miss Tyndale that dealt the final blow.

She rose at last, very much on her dignity, and went to her room to don bonnet and gloves and pick up her embroidered silk reticule. She descended the stairs with the dogged air of a prisoner approaching the block, but when Lawrence, himself now elegantly attired, handed her into the carriage, she felt a slight satisfaction at the way her eldest son had pressed and finally won his case. It was a victory she could understand.

Lawrence remembered well his sense of foreboding back in London when, at Tyndale Green, Lady Theresa tearfully informed them that Elena had not been seen all afternoon and Sir John, certain that something dreadful had happened, was at that very moment organizing a search party to comb every inch of the estate for her.

To his credit, Lawrence did not even bother to throw an "I feared as much" glance to his mother, who had greeted Lady Theresa with stiff formality.

Nor did he reveal his true anxiety beyond saying quickly, "May I offer my services in searching for your daughter?"

Lady Theresa assented in gratitude. "They are assembling in the servants' hall, I believe. Sir John has called on every able-bodied man. We fear a storm is brewing, and I am sure you will be a most welcome addition."

"If my mother could remain here with you . . ."

"Certainly. Won't you come this way, Mrs. MacLean?" Lady Theresa asked, ignoring the woman's glare at her son.

But Mrs. MacLean was furious with Lawrence for foisting her upon the Tyndale establishment this way. Her acquaintance with Lady Cunnington had not extended to the younger sister, and she had no idea what they would find to say to each other, given the awkward situation. Surely she could not admit that she herself had probably been the last one of them to see the wretched chit that afternoon.

"I dislike to intrude on your anxiety, Lady Theresa," she said. "Perhaps I had best await my son in the carriage."

"Not at all," Lady Theresa protested. "I should consider myself a most backward hostess if I allowed that. Besides, you must meet the Duchess of Malvern, who is visiting us."

Lawrence's mother pricked up her ears at this and allowed herself to be guided into the parlor. The Duchess of Malvern! Mrs. MacLean had long been an avid reader of all the Court news that appeared in *The Times* and *The Morning Post*, and the name of Malvern was not unfamiliar. The Duke had, for some years before the poor King's final madness, been one of his chamberlains, and the Duchess of Malvern, in her youth, had been one of Queen Charlotte's ladies.

She was both astounded and impressed that there could be such a connection between the Duke and Duchess and a simple baronet. It caused her to nearly forget her anger.

It disappeared altogether when the Duchess, seated next to Lady Cunnington in the parlor where they had gathered with Lady Theresa for moral support, extended a gracious hand to her and said, "Ah, Lord Harcourt's mother! So pleased. We became acquainted with him last autumn at Cheltenham."

It was impossible for Mrs. MacLean not to absorb a little of the apprehension the three ladies shared regarding Elena, even though her first unworthy thought had been, I hope the gipsies have kidnapped her. Now, her show of concern began to feel genuine. After all, if Miss Tyndale came to a bad end, Lawrence would blame *her* for driving the girl to it. She knew he would never forgive her.

She was not required to say much, for the others were too engrossed in speculation as to what might have happened to Elena to talk of anything else. At first Mrs. MacLean was lost in her own unhappy thoughts about the girl. But finally some of the conversation began to penetrate.

" . . . should have realized something was amiss when she ordered the carriage."

" . . . and Jane's statement that she wished to be by herself, even during the tea hour . . ."

And then the Duchess burst out dramatically, "I hate to say it, but one must come to the conclusion she no longer wished to live."

"Not wish to live?" Mrs. MacLean echoed, startled out of her brown study. "Forevermore, your Grace! Why should she not wish to live?"

The Duchess shook her head sadly and wiped an

eye with her frothy lace handkerchief, too overcome to speak more.

"She has certainly been distracted since our return from London," Lady Cunnington took up. "And I avow, with good reason. Those terrible rumors that drove her out of London . . ." She shook her head dolefully. "She had probably only just realized the full import of how they must affect her whole future." She glanced toward her former schoolmate. "I suppose you must know of them, Alice, for everyone else seemed to."

For the first time Mrs. MacLean was assailed with pangs of guilt. "Indeed, I had heard something of it," she murmured. "However, I was scarcely acquainted with your niece and knew not whether to disbelieve the *on-dits* or no."

"Like so much malicious talk, they entirely overlooked her basic goodness of character," the Duchess said firmly. "Anyone who knew Elena as I do would realize she could never do anything willfully and mortal or unkind. That is why it must have been such a dreadful blow to her."

"You seem very fond of her, your Grace," Mrs. MacLean managed. Her ears were suddenly ringing and her heart pounding. She hoped she was not having an attack of some kind.

"I am, I don't deny it. I even offered to adopt her once. Can't imagine why I was turned down." She threw a humorous glance toward Lady Theresa as though to divert her from the dread thought she had so recently voiced.

"My dear Genevieve, you have always enjoyed joking me," Lady Theresa retorted, her face set and white, "but I can scarcely consider it a jest when you suggest Elena could take her own life. I do not for one moment believe *that*."

Unless her hopes in another direction had just been dashed, Mrs. MacLean thought distractedly, compunction flooding her. How dreadfully mistaken she seemed to have been about the girl. But surely if someone of the Duchess of Malvern's stature could proclaim such unabashed admiration for her, it *had* been a mistake. If only it were not too late to make amends. . . .

She raised her formidable chin and said, into the pause that had fallen on them all, "Well, for my part, I am convinced your daughter must be safely found, Lady Theresa, for she has much to live for. I happen to know that it is the intention of my son, Lord Harcourt, to ask Sir John for her hand in marriage. With his consent, I shall be most delighted to receive her as my daughter-in-law."

19

Elena had wandered about the woods of Tyndale Green for hours, it seemed, pausing only now and then to wipe the relentless tears from her cheeks, thinking when she no longer wished to think, so unaware of her surroundings she had no idea where she had been or in which direction she headed. Now, with light fading in the overcast sky, she realized she was thoroughly lost.

She was also thoroughly fatigued—with emotion, with tears, with walking. The damp still air warned of a coming storm; the leaves of the trees all hung about her as though they had been severely chastened and awaited a sentence of death.

She felt equally chastened and condemned by the woman she had thought would become her mother-in-law. Now she wondered how she had ever thought Lawrence might overcome Mrs. MacLean's hostility to her. She was quite sure they could not marry in the face of it. Even if Lawrence returned with some plausible explanation for his sudden flight and his thoughtlessness, and still wanted her, even if . . .

But, of course, that had probably been the reason for his departure—his mother's opposition to their marriage. Not even Lawrence, determined as he was, could have prevailed over her determination. Elena recognized that Mrs. MacLean, despite her small stature, was an iron-willed woman, accustomed to ruling and being obeyed. She did not doubt she had convinced Lawrence that Miss Tyndale, with her tainted past, would never do as the wife of a viscount.

Whenever she reached this point in her thoughts, which circled over and over on the same tedious path to the same dismal ending, the tears would come. At last she slumped to the ground, heedless of the damage prickly weeds and the rough knobby bark of an oak tree could inflict on the apricot silk of her afternoon calling dress. For some time she remained motionless with exhaustion and despair. Even to move so much as a finger seemed beyond her.

What a strange thing love was! Three months ago, before Lawrence had come into her life, she had been resigned to living quite tranquilly from day to day on an even plane, relinquishing forever the dizzying heights and depths of the passion she had once experienced. But with a new taste of those heights an everyday sort of existence lost all savor. It seemed no better than purgatory, and there was no joy in any ordinary thing.

Lawrence, with his arms about her, his fascinating eyes glowing with love, his vigor, his laughter, his copper hair that caught and imprisoned the sun; Lawrence, *loving* her! She wished now she had been less prim and he less respectful, wished that she might have at least one consummation of their love to remember. A sweet surge of desire grew in her until it almost conquered her distress, and the thought of his rejecting her seemed incredible. If his love had been as strong as hers, could it have been so easily diverted by his mother's condemnation?

"We must have her blessing," she had insisted. That was before she had realized the depth of Mrs. MacLean's malice. Even if (oh, all those ifs, product of some germ of never-ending hope!) Lawrence had remained steadfast, even if he succeeded eventually in obtaining his mother's grudging acquiescence to their union, would she be able to find it in her heart to forgive the woman her devastating words of this afternoon?

When thunder began to rumble distantly, it took Elena several minutes to heed it. Finally alarm vanquished her numb despair and she realized she must bestir herself and try to find her way back. She rose and looked about with more concentration than before. Surely she could not be truly lost in her own familiar wood, which ran less than half a mile wide in most places. Yet not one tree or bush visible in the hazy twilight helped her decide whether she might be nearer the fen or the meadow, the river or the eastern end, where large posts marked the boundary of Tyndale Green.

It occurred to her that if she made some definite record of her progress—a broken twig or cut bark, she would not go about in circles, as she suspected she had been doing. Searching through her reticule, she found the small pearl-handled nail file she always carried with her, and started to scratch marks in the tree bark with its sharp point as she went.

The very air about her was darkening and the thunder broke more closely now, following flashes of lightning which she could sense rather than see. She heard occasional large plops spank the leaves high in the trees before she felt the first raindrop moisten her forehead. The wind came up suddenly, shiveringly cool. With an effort she conquered a strong impulse to rush mindlessly through the underbrush, seeking some fairy-tale shelter.

Then the rain came on swiftly, finding her despite the intervening leaves and branches. Even so she continued to meticulously mark each tree she passed, wiping raindrops from her face with her once-white gloves as she did so, and searching all the while for a familiar landmark.

At last—it seemed an age but couldn't have been more than seven or eight minutes—she identified a small clearing awash with tall grasses and ferns and clumps of blossoming meadowsweet, which were being torn and scattered by the wind and rain. She knew then that Old Will's cottage lay just beyond the next screen of trees and, beyond that, she would find the path that led home.

Rain lashed through her flimsy summer dress as she crossed the clearing. Espying the plastered walls of the thatch-roofed cottage, she ran through the last clump of trees and pounded on its door, intent on immediate respite from the growing ferocity of the storm. There was no answer. She fumbled open the latch with cold fingers and pushed desperately against the worn thick door until it gave way with a yawning reluctance. She darted inside, tardily hoping she was not interrupting some private ritual of Old Will's.

The cottage was empty. No fire blazed in the hearth, no candle welcomed her into its dusky interior. She stood with her back against the closed door after her first tentative calls elicited no response, letting her eyes become accustomed to the gloom. Her legs and arms ached from the sudden release of tension. She mopped her streaming face with the handkerchief from her reticule, but it was rather like mopping up an ocean. Her hair, matted to her head and face and neck, sent dribbles of water down her back, and her silk dress clung to her body in cold, sopping folds. She looked down in disgust at the ruin of her dress, her gloves, and her muddy, soaked shoes, and shivered. She couldn't just stand there, waiting for the storm to abate, but neither could she bring herself to go back outside and face it again. And it might continue for hours.

She looked about the room speculatively, trying to swallow a growing anger at her predicament, trying to concentrate on what she might do to prevent a racking cold from developing. The faint odors of tobacco, ale, and cooked cabbage mingled with that of age-dampened thatch. A long, well-used deal table held a jumble of pewter dishes and cutlery, and iron pots and kettles cluttered the hearth. An old wooden rocker near the cold fireplace seemed to be Old Will's one concession to comfort in the sparely furnished room. Beside it a tall three-legged stool held a stubby candle end in a black holder, a tobacco pouch, a large earthenware mug, and a dish cradling a half-smoked pipe.

She painstakingly peeled off her gloves and then her ruined shoes and went into the only other room. A small chest spilled clothes out of half-opened drawers, and jackets and leggings hung from wall pegs. Several kinds of shotguns and muskets ranged in a rack against one wall, and a cot with a large woolen blanket lying at its foot stood against another. Hurriedly—and with some impatience, for it was difficult to get at the buttons in back—Elena disrobed completely, rubbed moisture from her face and hair with an end of the blanket, then wrapped it around her. It easily spanned her height from shoulders to ankles, and the thirsty wool quickly absorbed the dampness from her body.

THE UNWELCOME SUITOR

In spite of its warm relief, anger arose in her again as she paddled back, barefoot, to the other room to look out a window. She had no idea where the gamekeeper might be—possibly caught in the storm like herself and forced to take shelter elsewhere. No doubt it was a blessing he had not been here, when she had been forced to strip herself naked, but what was she to do now? And what could they be thinking of her absence back at the house? The whole situation was disgusting and ridiculous.

All because she had allowed herself to be completely blue-deviled by a man's broken promise. Having only her father as an example, she had not realized what wretches men could be, and how untrustworthy. First Rodney, and now Lawrence: one of them involved in the most abominable deception; the other full of glib promises which, she was now beginning to suspect, he had never intended to keep.

That thought, which hit her with a sudden blinding clarity, put her whole dilemma in a different perspective. As she thought back now to the last time they had met, her anger reinvigorated her like a refreshing wind, driving away self-doubt, coloring every memory. Had he hoped to only *seduce* her in the abandoned pavilion overlooking his palatial home? Had he considered her all along a woman who had compromised herself and who was, therefore, fair game? It began to seem likely. He had halted his increasingly intimate caresses only because of her protests; then, no doubt, it had been only to prove his good intentions that he had been bamboozled (against his better judgment) into a proposal of marriage.

It had been his first and only real proposal. She could not count the morning in Hyde Park when he had referred so scornfully to her future intentions.

She doubted now, in her anger, that he had ever hoped to marry her, but she did not doubt he had always expected to possess her. Knowing she had been virtually another's mistress, he might have thought at first that she would be an easy mark. But he would not have considered her a likely wife. Only she, in her ignorance and naïveté, had supposed his intentions must be honorable.

The intriguing Lord Harcourt! That encounter in Cavendish Square when his boldness had been beyond belief. "I shall dare almost anything to make you mine," though they had met scarce four times. Incredible words. They made her shiver even now. They had declared he wanted her—but not that he would marry her. And his persistence! Despite her attempts to discourage him, he would not cry off. Gentlemen did not behave so to ladies they really respected.

What might have sent great waves of shame cascading over her an hour before now only provoked her to further disgust. They (Rodney and Lawrence had combined into one antagonist in her mind) had no right to treat her thus. No right to assault her virtue under pretext of marriage; no right to ravage the accepted rules of an ordered society in the exalted name of love; no right to win her heart with tender glances and charming words and the intoxication of music and dancing, then discard her as they might last year's worn-out boots.

She had been right in one thing: she should have stood fast in her determination not to marry again, but for a different reason. Why follow one mistake with another just like it? If Lawrence returned to claim her now (but why would he?), she would take back the words of love he had forced out of her. Take

THE UNWELCOME SUITOR

them back and flee—to Vienna, to Switzerland, to Italy, anywhere so that she need never see him again.

She left the window, where the sight of the raging rainstorm had ignited an equal rage within her, for the rocking chair. Wrapped tightly in the woolen blanket, she rocked back and forth violently, absorbed wholeheartedly in her new decision to stand independent of men, to forget Lawrence and the pain in her heart.

Without warning the door was attacked and thrown open, and the object of her wrath stood there, dripping wet, his condition similar to hers of a short time before.

"You!" she cried, jumping to her feet.

"Elena! Thank God! We have been looking everywhere . . ."

Lawrence removed the hat and cloak that had imperfectly protected him, threw them to the floor, and started impulsively toward her. He had halved the distance between them before he realized she was not responding in joyous greeting but had actually retreated from him and stood motionless, stony-faced and disheveled, clutching a large brown blanket tightly across her bosom.

He halted, frowning. "What happened to you? Where have you been?"

"Where have *you* been is more like," she countered coldly.

"Elena!" Hurt and surprise darkened his voice. "Well, of course . . . I'm most dreadfully sorry. We had word Lambert had run off from Eton after being disciplined. Mother was beside herself and insisted I investigate immediately, in person. I forgot . . . You have every right to be angry," he conceded anxiously, for she had not relaxed a muscle.

"And I am. Between your 'forgetting,' and the reception your mother gave me earlier today when I tried to learn what had become of you..."

"Oh, my love!" he cried out in compunction, and again started toward her.

"Don't you dare come a step closer!" She backed up again, until she felt the edge of the table dig into her back.

He stared at her in dismayed silence. "Have you so unforgiving a nature, then?"

"If you thought me willing to let you take advantage of me two mornings past, I warn you, I've changed colors. Unless you think it acceptable to violate the wishes of a lady simply because she was once tricked into a counterfeit marriage."

His eyes widened in understanding. "So you found out the truth about your precious captain."

"I found out, yes. And you knew all along, didn't you. You knew of his previous marriage. That was why you dared be so bold, why you felt justified pursuing me against my wishes, kissing me in a public park... And the other morning..."

"I knew of the marriage, that is all," he cut in. He took off his gray cutaway coat, its shoulders darkened with rain, and she realized he was dressed to the nines in a neckcloth once carefully folded, now drooping and starchless, brocaded vest, and ruffled shirtfront.

"Lord Harcourt..." she warned with renewed hostility.

But he simply placed the coat over the rocking chair and turned from her to the fireplace, where he began searching for a tinder box on the cluttered mantel.

"I should make some signal that I've found you," he explained. "Smoke from the chimney will give

THE UNWELCOME SUITOR 213

them a clue. We agreed this cottage would be a logical meeting point. Have you seen a lantern? We could put it in the window. Old Will is down along the dike by now, I expect. The others are searching the woods at thirty-yard intervals. Except your father. He was forced to go back to the house. The storm made it difficult for him to breathe and his valet quite insisted. I had arrived just as the search began, so I joined it."

He continued to explain how they had looked for her in a matter-of-fact voice, his back to her, while he took a bundle of wood and pieces of charcoal from the fuel box and arranged them in the grate. Then he struck the tinder and watched the flames take hold. She left off her mesmerized gaze and turned to look for an oil lamp, finally finding one in the bedchamber near the door.

She returned and handed it to him silently as he squatted before the new flames. As he took it from her, he seemed to see her exposed toes for the first time and his quick glance traveled to her face and away again with amused comprehension. She backed away and readjusted her covering more tightly, but it had begun to feel dreadfully scratchy and heavy. He lit the lamp with a taper from the fireplace, then set it on one of the window ledges.

"I'm sorry I've caused so much trouble for everyone," she said gravely to his back.

He turned abruptly. "What did my mother say to you?"

"She made it quite clear that she would never allow us to marry. And she's entirely right, of course. You cannot marry a woman with a sullied reputation. I was hen-witted to think it."

"You're quite out there—" he began.

"No, kindly permit me to speak. Even if you

wished it, even if you meant it and were not merely trying to get around me—"

"Get around you!" he echoed. "Damn it, Elena—"

"Even so," she continued inexorably, avoiding his eyes, "I could never be so selfish as to saddle you with a liability like myself. Or saddle myself with an implacable mother-in-law."

"Or a thoughtless husband," he put in.

"Oh, that's not to the point!" She whirled away from him, feeling her defenses crumbling.

"Of course it is! I should not have disappeared without explanation. If the world had caved in, I still ought to have made every effort to send you a message. That I simply forgot, in the stress of the moment, is inexcusable."

His self-condemnation did more than a hundred explanations could have done to restore her faith in him. She remembered then that, just as he had never tried to justify his part in Rodney's death by revealing to her the Captain's infamy, neither did he ever seek to excuse himself at the expense of others. Surely, in this case, he might have pleaded fatigue, too much on his mind, the urgency of the situation, his mother's importunities, but he had not.

The room was warming to the fire—or perhaps she was merely warming to his nearness, to the fact that he had come back, that there had been a reason for his absence, a good one, and she knew he could never act in any other than an honorable manner.

"Did you find him . . . your brother?" she asked, turning again to face him.

"Yes. The scamp had taken refuge in my London rooms after two exhausting adventurous days on the road. Elena, can't we just forget about . . ." His eyes glittered gold in the firelight, desire leaping in them like little flames.

THE UNWELCOME SUITOR

She felt trapped, vulnerable both to his need and to her own yearning, which had sprung to full life again. It was the latter that caused her to retreat again, this time the width of the room, and face him with anxious violet eyes.

"You have . . . You may take back your proposal of marriage if you wish. I won't blame you. I realize you probably did not originally intend to ask me."

"What utter rot is this? I have no intention of taking back a thing. I have hoped all along to win you —as my *wife*."

"Truly, Lawrence?" Her voice took on the incredulous, wistful tone of a child who had been read a fairy tale she could not quite believe.

He crossed the room impatiently, ignored the alarm in her eyes, and embraced her, blanket and all. "Elena, don't make me start all over again, for God's sake! I love you, I have loved you since I first saw you out near the fen. And I will marry you no matter what anyone says about *you*, or about my obligations to Society, or just the general unsuitability of the idea. There is no need for sacrifices!"

"I—you really ought to speak to my father first," she murmured, struggling against the attempt of his lips to imprison hers.

"I *did* speak to him before we began the search for you. Admittedly the thing was hurried and details left unsaid, but he seemed pleased and gave permission. Elena . . ."

His eyes pleaded that she put aside trivialities. His lips said the rest. Her own had hungered for his so long. Now they parted at his insistent pressure and fed on his silent promise, delighting in the cool, damp taste of him. He held her tightly, as if reining in his own desires, and the strength of his arms made resistance laughable and (perhaps fortunately) also made it impossible for her to abandon the blanket and reach up to touch his face and neck and hair, as she longed to do. Instead, she closed her eyes and sighed and nestled against him, still clinging to her covering.

His lips left hers to wander amid the damp ringlets on her forehead. "We're a rum pair, you and I," he said finally, laughter in his voice. "We must look like fugitives off a sunken pirate ship. I'd make love to you right now, on the floor, if I didn't think we'd be interrupted at any moment."

His outrageous words triggered a sharp tremor of excitement through her, but she forced herself to match his levity. "Then you misread me, for I have never thought I should like a fugitive pirate for a lover." The dimple in the corner of her mouth deepened, then was gone.

He kissed it and then released her to look out the window. "The storm is subsiding. I should alert the other searchers. We'll send for dry clothes for you and I'll take you back."

"Your mother . . ."

"Is in the parlor of Tyndale Green, talking to *your* mother and probably suffering pangs of remorse for the way she has treated you. She is not altogether implacable, you know."

"Can I really believe that?"

"You'll see," he promised.

Two hours later Elena accompanied her mother into the drawing room of Tyndale Green. She was wearing one of the new gowns she had acquired in London, of russet silk with insets of ivory Alençon lace in the bodice and skirt. A feeling of strangeness possessed her as she entered the room, as though she had been away for a long time or had suffered a

THE UNWELCOME SUITOR

lengthy illness. The carved arms and backs of the graceful Louis Quinze chairs, with their round plush or brocade cushions, shone with new luster in the candlelight. The pattern in the Persian rug Sir John had brought back during one of his travels to the East seemed brighter and more distinctive than before. It was, Elena thought, because she had been purged by despair and redeemed by love, all in the short space of a single afternoon.

Once home, she had been tenderly taken in hand by Jane, bathed and dressed and fussed over, and given a hot toddy laced with brandy to fortify her against taking cold. Perhaps it was the brandy that made all the people not quite real and, at the same time, uniquely precious to her.

Her eyes went first to Lawrence, who stood at the far end of the room in Sir John's borrowed cutaway coat, talking to the Duke. All eyes had turned on her and she knew the formal announcement of her engagement to him was forthcoming. She looked, with some reluctance, to the small gray-haired woman sitting on the sofa beside Aunt Winifred. Seeing her glance, Mrs. MacLean rose with a smile, came over, and kissed Elena on the cheek.

"My dear, we are so grateful you have recovered from your terrible experience and appear none the worse for it."

"Thank you," Elena said faintly, shocked beyond any logical response by Mrs. MacLean's turnabout.

Then Sir John escorted her to a settee near the fireplace, where Lawrence joined her. Like a scene in a play, she thought, dazed, every move seemed perfectly choreographed. Her father, standing tall and frail beside the seat, raised his voice, "My friends, as you may be aware, I have an important announcement to make . . ."

Afterward there were smiles and hand-clapping and exclamations of congratulation. Lawrence's formal kiss on her cheek set it glowing. Toasts were drunk with her father's best twenty-year-old Champagne, saved for just such an occasion. Then everyone milled about, raining on her more hugs and handshakes. But the only real presence was Lawrence, standing gravely beside her, his hand resting on her shoulder in warm reassurance.

Finally, after Eliot had announced supper and everyone began pairing off (Sir John handing down both Lady Cunnington and his wife), Mrs. MacLean came to Elena and said in a low voice, "I know you are surprised by my turn of mind, dear Elena. I must confess to having been dreadfully misled concerning your character, and I fear I must beg your forgiveness for certain hasty words of mine."

"Pray don't give it a second thought," Elena returned with a forced smile. "I certainly shan't."

"The Duchess of Malvern is the one who set me right," Mrs. MacLean pursued. "I know that anyone who has won such high regard from her must be beyond reproach."

"Indeed, madam," Elena agreed, her eyes starting to twinkle. "Of course, we all make mistakes in judgment from time to time. I am grateful for your blessing."

Mrs. MacLean drew back then with an almost audible sigh of relief, and Lawrence took each of them by one arm to escort them to supper.

"We suffer a lack of male escorts," his mother noted as they followed Sir John with Lady Cunnington and his wife.

"It will be good practice for you, Mother, to share me with Elena."

"Oh, I give you over to her entirely," Mrs. MacLean

returned tartly. "I shall have my hands quite full enough from now on with Lambert. Elena, my dear, you have rescued me just in time."

It was a moot question as to who had rescued whom, Elena reflected. Or who could claim the most credit for bringing her and Lawrence together. Everyone present could, no doubt, declare some small contribution. Her hand, which rested lightly on Lawrence's sleeve, impulsively pressed his arm. He looked down at her, surprised, and they smiled at each other, a secret smile full of promises, full of delight.

About the Author

After raising three sons and two daughters, Marjorie DeBoer turned her writing hobby into a career with the publication of her first historical novel in 1983. A graduate of South Dakota State University with a major in English-Journalism and a minor in Music, she has taught piano, violin, and public-school music. She continues to divide her time between piano and choral performance, and writing. She and her husband share their St. Paul, Minnesota, home with a Siamese cat and, on occasion, a hungry college-student son.

Don't go to bed without Romance!

- Contemporaries
- Romances
- Historicals
- Suspense

- Forthcoming Titles
- Author Profiles
- Book Reviews
- How-To-Write Tips

Read *Romantic Times*
your guide to the next
two months' best books.

44 page bi-monthly tabloid • 6 Issues $8.95

Send your order to: New American Library, P.O. Box 999, Bergenfield, NJ 07621
Make check or money order payable to: New American Library
I enclose $_____ in ☐ check ☐ money order (no CODs or cash)   RT
or charge ☐ MasterCard ☐ Visa

CARD #_____ EXP. DATE _____

SIGNATURE_____

NAME_____

ADDRESS_____

CITY_____STATE_____ZIP_____

Please allow at least 8 weeks for delivery. Offer subject to change or withdrawal without notice.

"THE ROMANCE WRITER'S MANUAL... A VERITABLE ENCYCLOPEDIA OF ROMANCE GOODIES."
—*Chicago Sun-Times*

HOW TO WRITE A ROMANCE AND GET IT PUBLISHED

by Kathryn Falk, editor of *Romantic Times*

Intimate advice from the world's top romance writers:

JENNIFER WILDE · BARBARA CARTLAND · JANET DAILEY · PATRICIA MATTHEWS · JUDE DEVERAUX · BERTRICE SMALL · JAYNE CASTLE · ROBERTA GELLIS · PATRICIA GALLAGHER · CYNTHIA WRIGHT

No one understands how to write a successful, saleable romance better than Kathryn Falk. Now she has written the best, most comprehensive guide to writing and publishing romance fiction ever—for both beginners and professional writers alike. From the field's top writers, agents, and editors come tips on:

- FINDING THE FORMULA: ROMANCE RULES
- SELECTING A GENRE: FROM HISTORICALS TO TEEN ROMANCE
- LISTINGS OF PUBLISHING HOUSES, EDITORS, AGENTS
- WRITING SERIES AND SAGAS
- THE AUTHOR-AGENT RELATIONSHIP
- ADVICE FOR MEN, HUSBANDS, AND WRITING TEAMS

"The definitive aspiring romance writer's self-help book... lively, interesting, thorough." —*New York Daily News*

(0451—129032—$4.95)

Buy them at your local bookstore or use this convenient coupon for ordering.
NEW AMERICAN LIBRARY
P.O. Box 999, Bergenfield, New Jersey 07621
Please send me the books I have checked above. I am enclosing $_____
(please add $1.00 to this order to cover postage and handling). Send check or money order—no cash or C.O.D.'s. Prices and numbers are subject to change without notice.

Name_____

Address_____

City _____ State _____ Zip Code _____

Allow 4-6 weeks for delivery.
This offer is subject to withdrawal without notice.

JOIN THE REGENCY READERS' PANEL

Help us bring you more of the books you like by filling out this survey and mailing it in today.

1. Book title:_____

   Book #:_____

2. Using the scale below how would you rate this book on the following features.

Poor	Not so Good	O.K.		Good	Excellent
0 1	2 3	4 5 6		7 8	9 10

	Rating
Overall opinion of book	_____
Plot/Story	_____
Setting/Location	_____
Writing Style	_____
Character Development	_____
Conclusion/Ending	_____
Scene on Front Cover	_____

3. On average about how many romance books do you buy for yourself each month?_____

4. How would you classify yourself as a reader of Regency romances?
   I am a ( ) light ( ) medium ( ) heavy reader.

5. What is your education?
   ( ) High School (or less)   ( ) 4 yrs. college
   ( ) 2 yrs. college   ( ) Post Graduate

6. Age_____   7. Sex: ( ) Male ( ) Female

Please Print Name_____

Address_____

City_____ State_____ Zip_____

Phone # (   )_____

Thank you. Please send to New American Library, Research Dept, 1633 Broadway, New York, NY 10019.

Other Regency Romances from SIGNET

(0451)

- [ ] **THE DIAMOND WATERFALL** by Sheila Walsh. (128753—$2.25)*
- [ ] **A SUITABLE MATCH** by Sheila Walsh. (117735—$2.25)*
- [ ] **THE RUNAWAY BRIDE** by Sheila Walsh. (125142—$2.25)*
- [ ] **A HIGHLY RESPECTABLE MARRIAGE** by Sheila Walsh. (118308—$2.25)*
- [ ] **THE INCOMPARABLE MISS BRADY** by Sheila Walsh. (092457—$1.75)*
- [ ] **THE ROSE DOMINO** by Sheila Walsh. (110773—$2.25)*
- [ ] **THE AMERICAN BRIDE** by Megan Daniel. (124812—$2.25)*
- [ ] **THE UNLIKELY RIVALS** by Megan Daniel. (110765—$2.25)*
- [ ] **THE SENSIBLE COURTSHIP** by Megan Daniel. (117395—$2.25)*
- [ ] **THE RELUCTANT SUITOR** by Megan Daniel. (096711—$1.95)*
- [ ] **AMELIA** by Megan Daniel. (094875—$1.75)*

*Prices slightly higher in Canada

Buy them at your local bookstore or use this convenient coupon for ordering.

THE NEW AMERICAN LIBRARY, INC.,
P.O. Box 999, Bergenfield, New Jersey 07621

Please send me the books I have checked above. I am enclosing $_____
(please add $1.00 to this order to cover postage and handling). Send check or money order—no cash or C.O.D.'s. Prices and numbers are subject to change without notice.

Name_____

Address_____

City _____ State _____ Zip Code _____

Allow 4-6 weeks for delivery.
This offer is subject to withdrawal without notice.